Heroes and other stories

Heroes
and other stories

KARIM RASLAN

TIMES BOOKS INTERNATIONAL
Singapore • Kuala Lumpur

Neighbours and *A New Year's Day Lunch in Jalan Kia Peng* have previously appeared in *Skoob Pacifica Anthologies Volumes One and Two*. *The Mistress* has appeared in *Men's Review*.

Front cover: *The Discreet Charm of the Bourgeoisie* from the Wong Hoy Cheong Collection courtesy of the Singapore Art Museum
Back cover: Photography by Tara Sosrowardoyo

Cover design by Hikayat Media, Kuala Lumpur

© 1996 Times Editions Pte Ltd

Published by Times Books International
an imprint of Times Editions Pte Ltd
Times Centre
1 New Industrial Road
Singapore 536196

Times Subang
Lot 46, Subang Hi-Tech Industrial Park
Batu Tiga
40000 Shah Alam
Selangor Darul Ehsan
Malaysia

All rights reserved. No part of this publication may be reproduced, stored in a retrieval system or transmitted, in any form or by any means, electronic, mechanical, photocopying, recording or otherwise, without the prior permission of the copyright owner.

Printed in Singapore

ISBN 981 204 695 X

For 'Tuah'

Contents

The Beloved 9

Heroes 22

A New Year's Day Lunch in Jalan Kia Peng 50

The Inheritance 73

The Mistress 80

Sara and the Wedding 88

Go East! 102

Neighbours 119

The Beloved

"*Sundal!* That's what he said about me. Me? Shukor, his wife – a *sundal*, nothing better than a bitch-dog on heat?" She spoke hurriedly and without introducing herself the moment I lifted the telephone receiver off the hook. I was still half-asleep but I noticed the line clicking as she spoke. She ignored the interference. I didn't. I rubbed my eyes and sat up.

"It's me. It's okay to talk, isn't it?"

"Yes." I said, not meaning it. I would have recognised Alissa's voice anywhere.

"I don't care. Shukor, he's treating me like dirt. The things he says about me – *gila babi*, and in public. Why did I do it, Shukor?" she said, her voice melting into a whisper. I knew it was for me to say something comforting but I couldn't and I remained silent.

"You must come tomorrow, to the Syariah Court, you must expose him – expose what he has done to me. Help me, Shukor, Shukor ... are you there?"

"Yes, I'm here." It was all I could say. I had learnt not to talk on the telephone.

"The Syariah Courts in Seremban at eight. Please! And call your other journalist friends. Let them see how the great Kamal Zamri, corporate chieftain treats his wife."

"I'll be there." There was a slight pause before she replied.

"You're the only one now, the others have deserted me. Even my mother and father." And she started sobbing.

"The bastards," I whispered under my breath, years of resentment exploding within me.

"I know, I know, you told me so. But you shouldn't have let me go. I know you still love me, Shukor. I've been reading your poems. If I'd only known, if I'd only thought ... you should have fought for me, hunted me down and saved me. Even if it was only from myself."

It was my turn to feel deflated.

"Alissa, *sayang*. Don't cry."

"You don't know what it's like – being watched all the time. He has his mother staying with me now – she listens to my calls and follows me day and night. The old bitch! I hate her. She's poisoning the children against me – telling them that I'm mad, unhinged. Me, Shukor? Oh no, I must go. I can hear his car. Shukor, I always loved you. Eight o'clock. Don't forget."

There was a final sullen click and the line went dead.

✻ ✻ ✻ ✻ ✻

I stretched my arm out and switched on the bedside light. It was four o'clock in the morning. Only four more hours. Rubbing my eyes I glanced at my wife. She was still asleep. She was used to me receiving telephone calls in the middle of the night and she hadn't stirred. Turning away from her, I reached out for my cigarettes, grabbed them, slicked one out of the packet, lit it and inhaled deeply.

Nooralissa Firdaus, the gracious daughter of Firdaus Rahman, the prominent businessman. Nooralissa Firdaus, the beautiful banker – *anak orang baik*, her *baju kurung* floating around her like the fine sand on the beach at Pangkor, whipped up by a sudden breeze. Nooralissa Firdaus, educated and charming. Nooralissa Firdaus, in the end, nothing more than the dutiful daughter and wife. The name 'Firdaus' in those days had been hallowed, weighty and important, something that would be mentioned in hushed, knowing tones. She'd also been 'Lissa' to her friends and 'Alissa' to me, because, as I'd explained to her time and again, 'We are lovers, not friends, Alissa – lovers.'

I mouthed her name silently, blowing cigarette rings as I did. I had loved Alissa more than I had ever loved anybody, including the sleeping presence next to me, a woman who had given me three children in quick succession without ever daring to ask me if I loved her. Alissa, on the other hand, had left me one day with nothing more than a crumpled *selendang* and a stash of her contraceptive pills. She had always demanded proof of my love: "Tell me you love me, Shukor. You're a writer, a man who uses words. Use them to worship me!"

She had been impossible and demanding, overturning and disrupting my life in her wake. I had once described her in one of my poems as being 'as capricious, if not as dangerous as the monsoon rains' and it was an image that was to haunt me thereafter with each year's torrential outburst. Like the rains, she timed her appearances with a faultless sense of drama, tantalising me as I waited. There would be deep banks of cloud, sudden telephone calls, a cool but disruptive wind, visits at midnight and then, ultimately, her body. Dramatic – it was always dramatic with Alissa. Arriving when you least expected her, she would become a maddening apparition – a torrent of life, a sudden tempest that would pass within a few hours, leaving no trace. When, as I half-suspected, she did disappear wordlessly and forever, she left a deep scar across my heart like a ragged gully carved by the rains in the baked-red hills above KL. A deep scar and a searing sort of pain that throbbed dully until it, too, subsided many years later and was forgotten.

I hadn't actively tried to forget her. Nor had I set myself the task of scrubbing her presence from my memories. It had just happened. Silently and without warning one day, the gully had collapsed in on itself and disappeared, which was strange really and contradictory too, because I had vowed both to myself and to the world at large that read my poetry that I would never forget her, ever. And, in fact, if anyone bothered to read my poetry it was still as replete with references to my lost love – though maybe not my lost Alissa – now as it had been then, some six years before. In fact, all my poems – the ones published in *Dewan Sastera* from the *Kekasihmu* collection – had been about her and no one else. Some of them had been written as recently as six months ago. I stubbed my cigarette out and swept away the ashes that had fallen on the bedclothes. Who and what had I been writing about all these years?

I was troubled by the question and what it seemed to suggest about my motives. Had I been as callous and selfish as Alissa? Had I, in fact, used her? I got out of bed, turned the bedside light off and walked out of the bedroom. I had converted one of the bedrooms of my terrace house into a study. It was my private refuge from the family – a place where I could work without being disturbed by the children. A place where I could forget the newspaper for a while and concentrate on my real love – my poems and my short stories. The air was stuffy inside the room and the glare of the fluorescent light stung my eyes. Sitting at my desk, I pulled out one of notebooks from the shelf and flicked through its pages, counting, as I did, the number of times the name 'Alissa' appeared.

*****

At first, I used to think about Alissa all the time. I'd see her face reflected in every shop-window and mirror I passed, smelling her scent in the night wind. But that was six years ago, you see? I'd see her face in the newspapers, usually in the social pages or I'd spot her husband's car parked outside one of the hotels – he had one of those single-digit number plates (rich bastard) that you don't forget. But I never saw Alissa. I liked to think it must have been the same for her, in a way. She would have seen my by-line in the newspaper and watched how my articles moved from the inside to the front pages; from vegetable prices, school open days to politics and foreign affairs.

In the days before she disappeared from my life, she had always been 'sunny'. And I don't mean 'sunny' in Malaysian sense – our sun cracks the back of your head like a shovel. She was 'sunny' in the New Zealand sense of the word (or at least what I imagine it to be since I've never been to New Zealand). She was bright and yet soft; warm and delicate – like those Salem 'Cool Country' ads that they repeat on the television hour after hour. I remember thinking that fate had really smiled on her: she was beautiful, she was rich and she was lovely. Her bank staff adored her – 'She's so good,' they'd say admiringly. The *jaga kereta* boys fought to look after her car and even the cut-fruit lady gave her extra portions of her favourite unripened mango. Blessed, I guess she was blessed. I had watched her during those months and soaked it all up like a sponge. Each night I was away from her I sat down at my desk and wrote – filling up notebooks with observations, phrases and sketches as if I was, as I knew I, in fact, was, a temporary visitor to another world – a world more rarefied and enchanting, where the air was sweeter and more succulent.

Whatever I professed to have felt and thought about her in my poetry, I saw that in reality I had hardly bothered myself with the woman. Alissa, my Alissa, had been nothing more than a resource. I had had my revenge for her sudden disappearance. Mining the 'pain of separation' like a thick motherload of tin ore was quite different from actually thinking of her, dreaming of her and talking about her. I had plundered my memories of Alissa and pushed the woman aside like the raw tailings at a tin mine. Now, after six years apart, I had to consider whether the woman was still as important to me.

It wasn't as if I'd completely forgotten her. There were stirrings. She was vague memory I would encounter if I passed the law courts. I'd feel something inside, as I drove past the lawyers in their gowns, something tender in the way that old, unhealed wounds always are tender – sensitive and painful if touched. However, there were times when the memories I had tried so hard to suppress escaped, flooding my thoughts. Then, in a sudden rush, I would be inundated by her, her smile, the way she'd push her brown hair behind her ears when she was nervous, the small scar under her left breast and the way she'd eat chicken, cracking the bones to get at the marrow. But

I'd shake thoughts out of my mind with a shiver, light up a cigarette and try to think of something else.

She had also made me promise that I'd never write about her – a bond that I'd broken almost immediately.

"Me? I'm irreducible!" she'd said at the time, laughing as she threw back in my face with an impertinent tilt of her head, a word I'd used only minutes before.

"I can use big words, too, Shukor but that doesn't make me a writer. Besides my life is going to be so boring that no one will ever want to write about me. I'll marry well – no, not you, you're too poor. I'll have three children and attend lots of charity teas with all my sisters."

But that was six years ago, before she had been plunged into a loveless marriage, betrayed by the man she left me for, the man her family had chosen for her in their wisdom – in their infernal pride and stupidity more like it.

In those days she laughed at me whenever I talked about my literary ambitions, my stories and my poems – it was never very pleasant when she was in one of her moods. I was junior reporter then and she was a creature of privilege for whom the words 'junior' and 'subordinate' were an aberration. She could be dismissive if she wanted to be, switching off, just like that, with a snap of her fingers as if I didn't exist.

*****

We were lying in bed at the time. In those days we spent most of our time in bed – you always do when things first begin, it's like a mad compulsion, a disease that can only be cured when you're naked and together. I used to think that we were no different from young lovers anywhere else in the world.

Later, I learnt I was wrong. I never wanted to spend so much time with anyone else thereafter. I wish I had, my life would be far easier. But there's never been anybody who even remotely equals her and I last slept with her six years ago.

Alissa was picking at the hairs on the back of my neck and tickling me at the time.

"Johari, I never want to be in one of your stories."

"Why not?" I replied, a little hurt. I had told her so much about my work that somehow I had hoped that she, too, would have been swept up in my dreams and carried along by their craziness. I wanted her to have enough belief in me to carry me through my doubts – a writer needs a muse, but more importantly he needs someone who believes in him. Someone who'd kill for him and his work. At the back of mind I thought that if she was that woman I could achieve anything. And foolishly perhaps, I thought she'd be that woman. I was such a fool. I should have known better because she had this capacity to hurt by her capriciousness. She would smother me with her love one day only to disappear the next for days and then weeks on end.

"I don't want," she'd say to me, "to be an unfinished character in an unfinished plot stumbling my way through a story that never ends. My life is planned: it's all fated. Ordered and ordained. I even know where I'm going to be buried.

"Everything must have a beginning and an end. I couldn't bear being stuck in one of your stories or poems." She shivered. She never changed her mind, never wavered even when I promised that I'd finish the story that I wrote about her.

"Like all the others?" she asked incredulously, pointing at my unfinished notebooks stacked along the shelf. I never mentioned the subject again.

But that was six years ago and she's married now with children or, should I say married 'off'. It all happened so suddenly: we were together making plans for the future, talking about kitchens and homes when she disappeared for a week – an unexplained absence that was followed by another and then another, until her absence became so commonplace that her presence was more of a surprise. It was as if she was a form of half-life, a disembodied presence that grew fainter as the weeks progressed. She vanished from my sight but not from the sight of others. My poor sweet thing. I loved her so much and she loved me – I know, but she fought against it because she knew she couldn't or rather that she shouldn't love me. There were other plans for her.

I know what you're going to say, that I'm a writer – that writers are always guilty of hyperbole, of exaggeration, lying through our teeth so that our stories will sound better, stronger, more melodramatic. I know, I've heard all the criticism before – that we're crass egoists, self-obsessed and selfish, twisting events and characters into a mould that makes us look better: damning those that damned us. But with Alissa it was true, it happened like that. It was as if I had taken a step into a cheap RM2 paperback melodrama and was playing out a role – the discarded lover – that was written by someone else. God, how I wished it had been my story. Then, at least I could have changed the plot, deleted the characters, altered their motives, their concerns and made myself a Tengku, a politician or a businessman. Anything but a bloody journalist! Shit! If only I had been a wretched Tengku – with a sneer, a *cicak*-like moustache and pockets wedged full of cash. Then she would have been mine, all mine and it wouldn't have taken much, just a little editing.

My mother says *'tak jodol'*, that it wasn't destined, that our love was ill-fated. She says that now but at the time she was ecstatic: she told half of Malacca and virtually all of Alor Gajah that I was going out with Alissa after I had brought her home just the once. Within a week she'd already chosen the *baju* she was going to wear for the *bersanding* and who was going to be my *pengapit*, worrying herself half to death, trying to figure out how she would carry herself when talking to Alissa's parents. They're so rich, so sophisticated, she'd say. It wasn't a serious worry, it was more a delicious kind of 'worry', the kind that occupies your mind for hours pleasantly.

Well, my mother says it wasn't fated now. But I know it was because I do. Every man knows these things instinctively. You don't stumble onto your destiny and remain unaware. And no, it's not like in the films where the hero's actions are accompanied by music and the plunging orchestrations of a thousand violins. That's just for the Bogarts and Bergmans, the P. Ramlees and Salomas. Even for writers it can seem pretty ordinary and banal. But when you're experiencing it, it's a moment of heart-stopping perfection, a moment so sharp and clear that your memories taunt you for years after with their vividness. A strange masochistic compulsion forces you to relive them again and again until your head spins with her scent in the air, the softness of her skin and the quiet sadness of her face in repose.

I was a scholarship boy from Alor Gajah and she the rich man's daughter. And she wasn't just any rich man's daughter. There are a lot of them hanging about at the Royal Selangor Golf Club practising their English accents and playing with their Chanel bags. She wasn't one of them because she had wealth and class. Her family had been rich and powerful for generations. They were everywhere, literally. Cousins in advertising, the law, banking and politics like most of us have pimples. The gap that divides now doesn't seem so wide or so unbridgeable. But then it seemed vast and impossible.

Well, I was the scholarship boy in his first job, reporting for the papers and she a lawyer. Maybe if my family had had a bit more money and seen a bit more of life than the Stadhuys in Malacca, they would have set their sights higher. Maybe I would have become a lawyer. Maybe then I might have been good enough to meet her parents and her family. Maybe ... but I think unlikely. I was never even remotely suitable and that was why she chose me – because she knew she'd never have to consider me seriously.

We met around the time when the law courts were a centre of political turmoil, a time when judges rushed from chamber to chamber, bewigged and scared, afraid for their jobs, their pensions and their chauffeur-driven Mercedeses. The older journalists used to lay bets on which judge would be suspended at any one time, a High Court sweepstakes that I found offensive at the time, though not any longer. The battle seemed so important then, the sort of thing that would have kept Alissa and I up until the early hours of the morning arguing: she was as passionate in bed as she was in her arguments.

We were both of us at the back of one of the courtrooms as some landmark decision was being made. The room was packed with lawyers, journalists, onlookers and thugs. I noticed her immediately, she was wearing a silk *baju kurung*, one of those long flowing ones that are made from expensive imported Italian silk, the ones that drape across a woman's body like gossamer. You know the kind of thing: it floats behind a woman as she walks, not like the awful nylon rubbish my sisters wear. For a poor boy like me she smelt rich from twenty yards. She could afford to be generous with her expensive scent whereas my sisters had to eke out their tiny bottles of cheap Javanese scent for months on end.

She was the most glamorous thing I'd ever seen. And yet, despite the dress and the groomed hair, her expression was serious and intelligent. She pursed her lips (she had full lips) as the judges delivered their judgment, shaking her head angrily. She had dark-brown hair that glowed even in the harsh fluorescent light. It was pulled back off her high-domed forehead and held in place with a velvet headband. She was perfect, like a doll, an intelligent doll.

She seemed to know one or two of the other journalists and I watched her as she sidled up to a well-known columnist and whispered in his ear. She wasn't gossiping or passing the time of day – she had something serious to say about the judgment and he nodded as she spoke, agreeing with her.

As I watched her whispering into his ear, her lips moving silently and swiftly, I tried imagining what it would be like to have this perfect creature so close to me, pressing herself against me and whispering in my ear. I could feel her hot breath and her breasts against my shoulders. Fascinated by her, I watched her closely: watching her slip through the crowd, watching her biting her lower lip and then wetting it. Having observed her for much of the morning I, too, pushed my way through the crowd and took up the place next to the columnist. Under the pretext of getting information I asked the columnist to introduce me to her. He sniggered but said yes. So it was, that I was introduced to her, "Nooralissa, this is Johari Samad, a journalist from *The Herald*."

She nodded and then carried on talking to the columnist, ignoring me as she spoke.

"... as my father says, the main issue now is not the judges but the judiciary itself – whether or not it'll survive. They're happy enough to see it die and the traditions thrown away."

"I'm afraid you're right," he replied.

"And what are you doing about it? You're all just toadies. Especially your newspaper, Encik Johan, your's is the worse – vicious slander is what you publish." By now she had turned to me and though she was speaking in a subdued tone her words were – each one of them – as biting as a slap across the face.

"I am just the journalist ... I don't control what the paper says. I wish I did but I don't. Besides my name is Johari." And I stopped, a little taken aback by the sharpness of her attack.

"I am sorry," she replied. She was more conciliatory now. "I didn't mean to be rude. Anyhow your editors should be shot!"

"Young lady, you're too outspoken for your own good." The columnist said to her quietly, "The walls have ears."

"So what?" and she swept her hand across her forehead imperiously. I was impressed. The woman was sexy and she had 'balls'. And that was how it all started – in a courtroom. We had both of us sensed an interest, that sliver of sensuality and mutual interest – the way she touched her hair and my desperate fumblings with my notebooks. We knew, though we pretended otherwise. I asked for her name card, she nodded and gave me one. She didn't ask for mine. She knew I'd call and I did.

We met, had dinner and that was how it all started. I borrowed a friend's flat – she said she couldn't ask her friends – and we slept together. At first it was perfunctory, almost desperate, like animals. However, as the months passed, our lovemaking slowed and became more gentle, though curiously enough, never loving. It was as if she had decided to be as craven as she in fact felt – seizing her pleasure with a fierce, desperate relish. It was only much later that I now realise that she was having her fill before the fall, before the court cases, the divorce and the betrayal.

The memory of her in bed with me, once revived, was still as raw as it had ever been. Sitting there all alone in my study, I felt the blood surging through my veins as I remembered, in turn, her face, her neck, her breasts, her stomach, her arms, her sex, her buttocks and her legs. My Alissa, all mine at last. The thought was intoxicating, heady even and I shivered despite the humidity. I could divorce my wife – that would be no loss, and be with Alissa, reunited at last with the sole object of my affections. She would have some money and together we could get a house somewhere outside of KL – somewhere like Janda Baik – and we could live as we were fated to live: together.

My head throbbed with excitement. At last the real Alissa and not some dusty memory. The woman herself. I paused. I had decided. I knew what I wanted. I would have Alissa. She would be mine. I would live with the single largest source of all my inspiration. She, who had inspired me to so much. The prospect of what she could do for me if we were living together was staggering.

I checked my watch. It was half past five already and I could catch some sleep before I got to the courtroom at eight. Turning my light off, I smiled. Alissa, Alissa, the prospect of the woman in the flesh had made me unaccountably happy, like a small child. I slipped back into the bedroom, pulled the thin cotton blanket over me and fell asleep almost immediately.

*****

I woke up at ten o'clock the next morning. It was my day off from *The Herald*. I didn't go the courtroom. Nor did I ever hear from Alissa again, though there were a series of strange, silent telephone calls in the middle of the night. I saw her photograph in a Malay language tabloid – the strained portrait of a woman under siege before she was taken away to Tanjong Rambutan for psychiatric evaluation. A writer lives life for his writing. Courage, love and steadfastness are for the world of poetry and fiction. They're not for real life. The two are different, at least that's what I try to tell myself, now.

Heroes

When Fariza, my daughter, was a little girl we'd play a game we called 'Are-you-sleeping?'. I don't know who thought it up. It might have been Fariza because she was always very inventive – even then. The game was enough to keep both of us entertained for the half-hour or so it took my late wife, Naimah, to prepare my dinner. We played it in the evenings – just as the heavy stillness of the night air pressed down against the windows.

Our game was very simple: I would leave the bedroom for a few seconds, returning silently whilst Fariza pretended to be asleep on the bed. As she slept – lying on her back, or at least pretended to be asleep – she was supposed to watch me through her half-closed eyes. If I managed to tickle her on the stomach before she saw me I would win. If I didn't then she would win. It wasn't particularly complicated but we both enjoyed it. She trusted me so much that one night I turned the light out in the room and she wasn't frightened at all. I guess all daughters adore their fathers and Fariza was no exception.

She would squeal with pleasure whenever I managed to tickle her. In between the laughter, she'd cry out, "Ayah, Ayah, you win! You win!" Sometimes she'd be so animated she'd scream out loud. Daughters! The memory still makes me shake my head. In those innocent days I would rush home to spend all my time with her.

✧ ✧ ✧ ✧ ✧

We were a small family, just the three of us: Naimah, myself and Fariza and we lived in one of those single-storey bungalows with green louvre windows on the edge of Petaling Jaya's Section 5, just beyond the shadow of Gasing Hill. Naimah loved Section 5 from the start. She adored the nearby shops – just a short walk away – the efficient if punctilious Chinese *dhobi*, the banana-leaf restaurant where the waiters called her Kak Naimah and gave her extra large, crunchy *wadeh* and the Hock Siow's General Store where they sold Cadbury's chocolate, Jacob's cream crackers and fresh *kangkong*.

Our garden was spartan, if not desert-like. I had limited funds and couldn't afford the luxury of a gardener. Naimah, for her part, didn't like flowers and plants (she didn't like to get earth under her nails). Having said that, we did plant a mango tree in the middle of the front lawn. Sadly, it withered when we forgot to water it during the drought of '68 and the Labrador bitch from the house next door seemed to enjoy urinating over its roots so much that one day when Fariza leant against it, it keeled over, never to recover.

The interior of the house, however, was quite the opposite. If the exterior was a desert, the interior was a jungle by comparison. Naimah loved housekeeping and sowing. As a consequence we had a surfeit of brightly coloured soft-furnishings. There were curtains hanging in all the windows which was very unusual in those days. She had also made a set of twelve cushions covered in peach-coloured Thai raw silk. Naimah was very proud of her handiwork, just as I was proud of her. She was thrifty, buying the silk with money she saved from the housekeeping allowance and paying in a specially negotiated series of monthly instalments from a shop in the Weld supermarket. In many ways she was as careful with our money as I was with my behaviour in public and my language.

We had a set of rattan armchairs with hard foam cushions in the centre of the living room. There was also a small nest of metal chairs strung with brightly coloured plastic for Fariza and her friends. Opposite the rattan armchairs was a large Phillips radio-television console that squeaked whenever we opened it. The console had been our most expensive purchase and we treasured it for many years. The floors downstairs had been laid with terrazzo tiles and since it was always so hot in the middle of the day the cool dark-blue terrazzo was a pleasant respite from the sun's glare. In fact, some nights when it was just too stuffy upstairs the three of us would camp out on the sitting-room floor under the whirring blades of the overhead fan. We rolled out *mengkuang* mats and slept with an array of bolsters, pillows and cotton blankets. Fariza would insist on a special mosquito net for herself. Since I was an indulgent father, I would hang one up over her, suspending it like an inverted spider's web as she danced around under it like a excited rag-doll. In retrospect it was a wonderful time.

Marrying late in life, Naimah and I only had the one child, Fariza, our jewel. I thank Allah that he allowed me to enjoy the blessings of fatherhood. Conversely, I shudder to think of what I would have missed had Naimah and I remained childless – especially now. After my wife's death and in the lonely hours of my bereavement, Fariza and her young family have been my sole source of solace.

Alone now in the same Section 5 house, I spend a great deal of my time sitting and dreaming of Naimah, the past and the three of us. Despite our straightened circumstances – we were always a little short of cash – it was all so perfect then, almost idyllic. Occasionally the memories are so fulsome and real they make me shiver. '69 might have been a terrible year for some, a scar on the nation and all that but for me it was a high point of sorts, a moment of rare harmony, a time when I was vigorous, capable, important and, if only to my lovely daughter, even heroic.

✦ ✦ ✦ ✦ ✦

Now that I have been asked to write this journal I should stop rambling on about the past and start at the beginning. I have never been particularly comfortable with words and those who use them for a living. In short, I don't like 'so-called' wordsmiths. They're just *tipu-tipu* merchants if you ask me. Locksmiths, carpenters and padi-farmers actually do something useful. Wordsmiths conjure nothing out of air. This may sound sweeping but I have my reasons: good sound reasons.

I am not and never have been a man of many words. I was always taught, as a civil servant, that those who used too many words were a danger not only to themselves but also to their colleagues and their country (expanding on Naimah's primary principle of thrift). They were the ones who were careless with their words, the ones who spread idle gossip and left silly notes strewn across busy desks. Over the years I was to see that it was these acts, or rather the signal failure to act, that were the true seeds of disaster and chaos – not deliberate evil. Inadvertence and neglect rather than malice. Fool's work, not Syaitan's as my *ustaz* would say.

Words, words, words. My mother used to say they were as dangerous as the teeth of a tiger. Maybe I'm superstitious and unduly old-fashioned, but unlike many people I know, I've always listened very carefully to such advice. I paid heed. I saved my words – storing them away religiously, even reverentially because I was aware at all times of the violent forces and destructiveness that lingered below their seductive euphony. In a strange way, I have always thought it appropriate that the Malay word for vocabulary is *perbendaharaan perkataan* – 'a treasury of words'. And because I was so particular and determined in my ways – saving, saving, always saving – I grew to amass the most extraordinary wealth of words. I became a hoarder of words. I was truly rich. However, there were times when this cornucopia of language left my head so heavy in the mornings I could hardly wake up because silence does have its drawbacks. In those days I used to have so many words, phrases, *pantuns*, sentences and speeches whirring around my head. I felt that I, alone, was the treasurer of all the words in existence – the guardian of all the dictionaries, thesauruses and *kitabs* in the world.

When I was in the MCS, I shunned the use of words as much as possible – writing the slimmest of reports and notes. Some of my superiors thought my ways exemplary whilst others, generally those who knew no better, criticised me for what they took to be laziness. But as I often told Naimah – the ones who know, know. Whereas the others, by definition, were not truly civil servants. *They* didn't understand the delicacy of writing a report – the need to be both precise and yet suggestive: clear and at times even opaque. I know that poets go on about their art, but I assure you that a well-crafted report is as much a piece of literature, if not more, than a clunking, badly-executed sonnet or a *syair*. After all, a report, so innocuous at first, can grow to haunt you, especially if your conclusions – often years later and with the benefit of hindsight – are proven to be incorrect.

I have known of men, prominent civil servants like Datuk Halim whose careers were hallowed and spectacular. All of a sudden a report is aired. Thereafter their careers are spectacular for their decline. Such tragedies! Tragedies that could have been avoided had they only thought to be a little more attentive, a little more circumspect. Just think of it? Tripped up by a hastily drafted, ill-thought through report decades before.

As you can see, this doesn't mean that I don't like language, because I do, though I know that Fariza, who is a journalist, thinks otherwise. It's just that I understand, or rather I respect, the power and authority of language too much to employ words in any way which is inaccurate or sloppy. Some of my colleagues deliberately misinterpreted me, however. They accused me of being an Anglophile, a lover of the British and the Chinese. Whispering behind my back they said that I was an elitist, a feudalist and therefore disloyal to the Malay race. They didn't see, or rather they didn't want to see, that the use of language – any language – requires both courage and intelligence: the courage to forbear and the intelligence to know just when to desist. A fool wielding words whether they be in Malay or English can reduce the world to tatters and chaos. Look at Datuk Halim!

All of which is ironic given the fact Fariza who I love more than life, *is* a journalist by profession – a tribe of men and women who are notorious for their disregard of the sanctity of language. Even now, and I'm seventy eight, I hate to think of travesties committed in the name of 'the news'. Hah, such rubbish! As if these still-drooling little children masquerading as men and women of the world are so very important and so very clever. Courageous truth-seekers and seers, so she tells me. But they know nothing of the complexity and intricacy of government! How can they be the judges when they themselves have never known the difficulties of running the country. Let them run the country for a while and then let them complain!

And it was whilst I was in one of my periodic rages, castigating the press for their ignorance and presumption, that Fariza stopped me short. Pressing her forefinger to her cheek, just as she did when she was a child, she spoke. Her mother had been level-headed and calm at all times and Fariza had inherited her temperament as well as the ability to see through my bluster.

"Ayah," she said, her eyes fixed on mine, "if this is so important to you, then I think you should tell your side of the story. If it isn't important enough for you to write it down then it really shouldn't be important enough for you to get all angry about." In retrospect I don't know what I was more furious about. Was it my daughter's gall for interrupting me in mid-flow or the deftness with which she had cornered me – forcing me to concede that I should consign my story to pen and paper, something I'd refused to do for so many years.

"Alright, alright," I remember saying, half-forgetting my earlier rage, "get me a notebook and I'll start. I'll write – I'll tell my side of the story. I'll tell it all." She nodded in reply, a sly if victorious smile passing briefly over her face.

"Good," she said approvingly, "I'll buy the notebook today and you can start tonight. I know there's a great deal to write about. For a start, I want to know about that boy – Nazrin. He used to visit the house all the time in those days. I want to know why you were so kind to him. Mak used to say you were very courageous and brave in those months. I think it's time you told us about it." With that she made her excuses – she was late for work – and left, though not before kissing me gently on the cheek.

That evening, just as she had done every night since Naimah's death, Fariza came to the house with her daughter Mariam. In one arm she carried two large notebooks, a pair of those large Chinese ledger-like notebooks that seem to creak as you opened them, in the other her two-year-old daughter. She left the notebooks on the main dining table and placed her daughter on the floor. Ignoring the notebooks, she chatted with me as if nothing had happened earlier in the day. When, finally, I made a move towards them, I could see her half-rising from her seat in anticipation. The notebooks were much heavier than I had expected and I dropped them both. My hands, you see, are arthritic. The crash surprised Mariam who started crying immediately. Fariza ignored her daughter entirely and dashed up to me.

"Ayah!" she said quietly, her voice underscored with concern, "are you alright? I wouldn't want anything to happen to my hero, now."

"Oh, Fariza, without your mother I'm so useless," I replied in my frustration.

"No, you're not, Ayah. Don't be so silly. I love you."

I couldn't find the words to answer her. Instead I cried. Not as loudly as my granddaughter, but I cried. And as I sobbed, my daughter – a child that I had once cradled in my arms and thrown up into the air as readily as a shuttlecock – wrapped me in her warm, protective arms.

✦ ✦ ✦ ✦ ✦

Fariza was always an observant and sensitive girl. When Naimah, my late wife and I quarrelled she would fall silent and hide away in the garden as if afraid that she'd been responsible for the fight. At night, long after she was supposed to be asleep, she would knock on our door and tell us that there was a prowler in the garden or a stray dog outside the servants' quarters. We'd tell her not to bother, to go to sleep but she'd insist. Invariably, she was right as the next day's missing *cangkul* or overturned rubbish bins would prove.

She once found me handing over cash to a Malay boy who arrived in a taxi. As he stretched his arm out of the window to receive the cash, I looked around only to catch sight of her standing beside me pensively, staring at the boy.

"Ayah, why didn't the boy get out of the car?" she asked later. "That's very rude of him, you know?"

"He can't walk," I replied.

"I thought so. His face was too good to be a rude person's. I think he's a very loyal boy. Is he a hero too, Ayah?"

When on his fifth or sixth trip to the house, I found him talking to her, I reprimanded her and sent her inside the house. She started crying but I insisted. This was men's business, I told her. For the rest of the day she avoided me, sulking in the servant's quarters.

That evening after her bath she confronted me as I was reading the newspaper. She stood opposite me in her pyjamas with one hand on her hip, her face caked with *bedak putih*, and coughed into the back of her other hand before addressing me. I can still remember the concerned expression on her face as she spoke. She looked like a miniature version of her mother – a diminutive, slightly solemn housewife who was just about to reprimand a lazy servant girl. Pausing for effect, she only began speaking when she knew she had my full attention and as she spoke she rested her forefinger on her cheek.

"I will marry that boy from Perak, Ayah. He said his name was Nazrin and I love him. You must love him very much because you are so kind to him, so generous. And I can only marry a man that you love, Ayah."

Naturally, I was stunned by her statement and I tried to pass over the matter – ignoring her with a snort. But Fariza was adamant and for months thereafter she would talk about Nazrin as if he were her closest friend – 'Nazrin says I'm very pretty' and 'Nazrin said I looked very elegant in black'.

Understandably, I ensured she never saw him again. Nevertheless, she talked about him all the time – chirping on in her own sweet manner like a hummingbird as if the *nikah* was only a matter of weeks away. Thankfully, she returned to school when the schools reopened. And in the rush of school activities, Nazrin appeared to slip to the back of her mind. Thankfully, I say, because Naimah was growing a little concerned by Fariza's strange fascination with the boy, raising her eyebrows to me every time the name was mentioned in our presence, as if to say '*Padam muka*! Now look what you've done!'

A few years later Naimah forced me to tell Fariza that Nazrin was alright, now – that he could walk and that he was happily married with children. She looked shocked and though she never said anything to me she never mentioned his name until her own wedding day when she said just before the *nikah*:

"Ayah, I waited for Nazrin but he never came."

✧ ✧ ✧ ✧ ✧

Fariza has long pestered me to write about the past. When she says 'the past', I know what she really means. She wants me to write an account of May '69 – as if the events of those bloody weeks explain the decades that followed. I've been trying to tell her the past isn't just '69. 1969 was an aberration, a ghastly aberration and nothing more. I know some people think of it as the nation's defining moment, a terrible cry of despair. What nonsense! As if history and the march of time can be determined and charted so simplistically. Rubbish.

Personally, however, it was an important time for me, a time when I was entrusted with many onerous responsibilities. I had to make difficult, bold decisions, often at odds with my training as a civil servant. Fariza was a small child at the time, nothing more than a mere chit of girl. What could she know? Though I can remember her perfectly well. I can still recall quite vividly the day when the first of many armoured cars pulled up in front of the house, summoning me to the Operations Centre. She was wearing her playshorts and a simple tunic. I think she waved as I clambered into the car, swallowed up by a gun-metal green apparition.

Could it be that she saw the shimmer of excitement in my eyes, the pride and the honour? Maybe. Perhaps Naimah mentioned the incident to her? Could it be that Naimah told her about all those long, silent curfewed nights that I was away formulating, discussing and organising for an eventuality that never in fact happened? Of course, I've never, ever said anything to Fariza. Not that she hasn't asked. She has. Each time I have deflected the question and evaded giving an answer. She thinks I was a hero or saviour of some kind, which is true to a degree. We were involved in something very major, an undertaking that was to make a vast difference to our country and our people.

There are times when I suspect her desire to become a journalist was born from the confusion of those months. Certainly, I have never encouraged her interest in the local press or journalism. In fact every morning for as long as I can remember, I have read the local papers and shuddered at the terrible abuse of language, grammar and syntax. And this isn't just in the English newspapers alone – the Malay press is just as culpable. Of course, my daughter's views are more robust than my own. She tells me a newspaper's responsibility is to report the truth – the whole truth and nothing but the truth. Good grammar, so she tells me, is for the pedants. *Astagfirullah*! Doesn't she realise that sloppy writing means sloppy thinking! Without form the substance is mere gibberish – *sampah*! How can bad English ever be excused? Besides, if everyone knew the truth there would be chaos. But children, especially one's grown-up children, become like strangers over the years, the fact of their birth and infancy as distant as a dream.

So here I am writing a journal for my daughter and my granddaughter, a journal she has insisted that I write because as she says, 'it will be many years before Mariam can talk to her Dato' as an equal and I want her to be able to enjoy the full benefits of your wisdom and experience'. Those were her words, not mine. I would never want my granddaughter, Mariam, to talk to me as an equal. But, as I said, she used all her wiles and canniness to force me into doing exactly what she wanted.

She wants me to write about my days in the administration and especially that troubled year. I have told her time and again that those are precisely the incidents and episodes that I cannot tell her about. We have argued but I have refused to concede. Part of the problem lies in the fact that her husband is not Malay. He is a Chinese and a journalist, too. Fariza tells me that it is solely in the interests of her daughter, whose racial ancestry, of course, is mixed that she has persisted in this matter – telling me discreetly but firmly that peace and reconciliation can only be achieved through truth.

Peace and reconciliation? Truth brings chaos, destruction and death. There are times when whole nations are happier subscribing to the great 'lie'. What about justice, destiny and domination? Leave the truth to the philosophers. Let them dissect it and pull it apart. Real people aren't bothered with the truth. They want results, they want homes, jobs, schools, electricity and water. That's the truth. Certainly we weren't concerned with the 'truth' except insofar as we tried to shroud the ugly 'truths' that were buried in men's hearts.

✿ ✿ ✿ ✿ ✿

Truth? What does she know? It still irritates me, even now. Truth? Only Allah knows the truth because only he can see into the hearts of all men. I, am not so privileged. Even my own heart is, at times, closed to me. It's hard to tell Fariza who believes in the innate goodness of mankind that the hearts of men and women are stuffed with evil. Their hearts are as full of evil and malice as *onde onde* is full of sticky, black palm sugar. Puncture the soft, appealing exterior and the palm sugar seeps everywhere, touching everything. No, man is evil. That's the truth. It's brutal and it's ugly but that's the incontrovertible truth. Take away order and he will steal, he will rape and he will kill. That's what '69 taught us – the truth about man's condition, that man is a beast at worst and a coward at best. But there again, Fariza was only seven when I was called to act for the good of the nation. What can she know? She who has grown up in a country where every year seems richer and more stable.

What can any of them know? I suppose I shouldn't be so harsh on them. They are all so innocent and trusting: believing what they want to believe. I have sat and listened to them talk. I've heard them but they're just children, mere children, their lives untouched by the pressures we faced in our day. They look at us and sneer. I look at them and pity them. For them, the *Malay Dilemma* is little more than a question of whether or not to take the money.

What if I wasn't a hero, I ask her? But she smiles blandly. She knows I am a hero and is therefore unafraid of the truth. Having heard stories of my involvement in those days, she presumes the best because I'm her father and she loves me. She presumes that I was brave and courageous. How can one's father be anything but brave? One's children seldom think otherwise. The first to revere you are sometimes the last to know.

That I acted for the good of the nation, I will not deny. I didn't act out of self-interest – the stakes were too great for selfishness, though some tried. It was a difficult time and there were enemies everywhere. We had to be harsh to survive, striking down those who would not agree with our vision of Malaysia. There were a few days when it looked as if my people, my race, would be wiped out. As I said, the stakes were high. In such an environment we had to be uncompromising and harsh. We had a burden, a mission which was all-important – the preservation of the Malay race – and to this end I was forced to crisscross the country, travelling at great speed from town to town carrying important messages, entrusted with great powers.

There were decisions we were forced to make that haunt us even now, decisions that I wished I'd never made. I stopped for no man because there was too much at stake, too many people's hopes and ambitions resting on my shoulders. I stopped for no man. I had to press on. Hang Tuah would have approved of me. I never questioned. I acted on instructions whatever the consequence.

❊ ❊ ❊ ❊ ❊

Fariza still wants to know more about Nazrin. She's not content with what I have written to date. She wants to know the facts. From the questions she's been asking and the way she's asked those questions, I understand – just as any father would, that she has some unfinished business to resolve. She wants to know who he was and why I was so good to him – sensing perhaps rightly that my courageousness lies in the silent mystery of that boy. She's pressing me for more, day after day. I've tried telling her that all stories must have their mystery, that not everything should be made known immediately, if at all. But she's as persistent now about the boy as she was in the first place about the journal.

Having agreed to this wretched journal I can't seem to control what I want to talk about. I'm being forced to tackle countless other subjects – subjects that I would prefer forgotten. Am I growing careless? Am I becoming the weak old man I always feared I'd become? Are my words beginning to assume their own momentum? Am I in danger of becoming as much a hostage to my language as Datuk Halim before me?

"Tell me, Ayah!" she implored last night. I felt embarrassed. I don't like to be seen to be blowing my own trumpet. Sometimes a story is better told by someone else.

"He was a young man I had to help along the way. He was one of the victims of violence. He was one of the unfortunate ones." Listening carefully, I saw that she was unconvinced.

"Ayah? I know there's more. I'll find out, you know? I am a journalist. We can hunt down the truth if we want to. I know you're being modest. I can tell. I'm your daughter."

"The truth," I said, "is hard to know."

✼ ✼ ✼ ✼ ✼

Fariza hasn't been to the house in days. Normally she visits the house everyday. I miss her and Mariam so much. When they're not around I feel only half-alive. In their absence, the garden and the house seem drab, the heat oppressive and my spirits are low. It all seems quite different when they're around. Finally, I called up her house but the servant said they were all outstation.

"In Penang," she said. The words made me shake.

"Are you sure?" I asked.

"Penang. Seeing Nazrin." I put the telephone receiver down abruptly and sat down. Suddenly my legs felt very weak. Every time the telephone rang subsequently I cringed inside, formulating to myself excuses, reasons – words, words, words.

Even my most treasured of memories seemed tinged by a note of sourness, no longer a source of comfort. Anything that reminded me of Fariza frightened me. It was impossible to even think of the game, our game without feeling short of breath and tired.

✼ ✼ ✼ ✼ ✼

I knew what I had to say. I knew what I had to do. I was entrusted by the highest authorities carrying messages of national importance. I was driven from one centre to another carrying the notes and comments that couldn't be sent in any other fashion. I had to be as loyal and dependable as the Sultan's private *Laksamana*. We were all afraid of letting these precious documents fall into the hands of the enemy – whoever that was?

I had strict instructions. Plough on! Don't stop! Faster! Always faster!

*****

Finally, after almost a day and a half of waiting, Fariza called on the telephone. Her voice was quiet – almost inaudible and pinched.

"I met him, Ayah. I met Nazrin. He's not better. He can't walk and he isn't married." She spoke quickly. Her voice was strained and cold. I could sense the pain as my innocent, unthinking deception, all those years ago, fell apart.

"I'm sorry," I apologised but she wasn't listening. She continued in a chilly monotone.

"He's very loyal, Ayah. Very loyal. Says it's all his fault. Says he still admires you, respects you. Your leadership, your devotion to the job, your sense of duty at all costs … his cost," she added ominously.

"I know, I know," I replied hurriedly, not wanting to hear any more. I could sense her antagonism on the telephone line.

"Ayah, his face, it's so beautiful, still – unlined and soft. What happened? Ayah, you're my hero. You let me down." Her voice tapered off.

"I'm so sorry," I said once again, hoping to sound suitably apologetic. "When can you come to the house? I want to see my Mariam."

"Ayah, I have to go to the in-law's tonight."

"But you always come to see me – every day," I wailed pathetically.

"I must go, Ayah. Bye."

"Fariza, the truth isn't always worth knowing. Don't leave me." As I sobbed – the sobs of a foolish old man – she replaced the receiver.

*****

This is going to be my last entry in this journal – a venture that I should never have undertaken. Let me tell you a story:

It was May 30th, 1969 and I was in north Perak on my way to Penang. It was just two weeks after the election and the air still seemed to hang heavy with hatred and the stench of dried blood. It was so bad in KL you could rub the tension between your fingers and smear it on the windows. In the aftermath of the fighting I had been entrusted with a special task, taken aside and briefed. A leather briefcase had been passed to me and, sitting in front of my superiors, clutching the briefcase like a child, I absorbed their instructions. I was to carry it to Penang, pass the contents to the Gerakan leaders and then, having let them read the contents, I was to open discussions with them. In short, I was an emissary. I was to be the conduit for discussions that were intended to be both frank and open: we had to stress that we had nothing to hide. Listening to my instructions, I nodded slowly. The responsibilities were great and despite my personal anxieties, I had to admit that I was enthralled by the prospect of running such an important mission.

Of course the reality of the mission was not quite so glamorous. The journey had been long and troublesome with roadblocks manned by swaggering policemen and soldiers. Because of my letter of authority I was accorded special treatment – soldiers stood to attention when they addressed me and policemen stuttered. On certain stretches we were given military escorts, on others, however, nothing. As a result there were times when we rattled along silent roads that still seemed to seethe with discontent and dissatisfaction.

Driving through the Chinese district of Menglembu past the hulking remains of tin-mining dredges being gutted and refitted, the air appeared to be charred and dangerous as if a single match could set everything ablaze once again. I stared out of the car and felt my heart sink as I watched shuttered shophouse after shuttered shophouse interspersed with barricaded homes, torched cars and a pack of wild dogs tearing at a pile of uncollected rubbish.

The atmosphere was forbidding. It was as if there was a common realisation that an abyss had been approached, an abyss that presented a desperate plunge into unending violence and brutality. The abyss seemed unavoidable in those early days and we passed on, reminded once again of the importance of our mission. Soon enough, however, we were out of Ipoh, hurtling along an eerily quiet stretch towards Sungei Siput. Generally, we tried to keep away from the towns, preferring the relative peace and emptiness of the open country. There, among the *kampung* Malays we felt safe.

There were three of us in the car. The generals at the Operations Centre had dubbed us 'The Three Musketeers'. One burly and rather disdainful Lieutenant-Colonel had added rather sourly that we were more probably 'The Three *Mus-tikus*', a comment that I chose to ignore. Many of us senior civil servants felt uncomfortable in the presence of generals and we observed them warily. Nonetheless they had been generous with me as regards the trip. I had been provided with a large Mercedes limousine. I sat in the back seat with the all-important briefcase, whilst Omar, my driver, and Nazrin, my aide, sat in the front seats.

Nazrin was a young fellow in his early twenties and straight out of Universiti Malaya. He was just the sort of young, bright Malay boy that we wanted to see prosper in new Malaysia, just the sort of boy that we were afraid would slip through society's net if we didn't help him. Every time I looked at him, and he was a pleasant-looking boy, I was reminded of the obstacles we, as Malays, had to overcome to empower our own people. I was reminded of everything that he had shirked off so effortlessly: the poverty, the ignorance, the feudalistic ways and the passivity in the face of change. He was remarkable young man.

Occasionally, however, my fears for the future of my race would leave me feeling hopeless. And then, looking up from my desk, I'd see Nazrin rushing around the Operations Centre, smiling eagerly, his face suffused with excitement. Watching him, I'd regain my confidence. If only there were enough young men like Nazrin, we had a future – a real future. I don't think he realised quite how much he became, at least for me, in those tense weeks a source of quiet inspiration and hope.

A Malay Studies graduate, Nazrin was enthusiastic and friendly, in the way that small town boys generally are. They bow lower than their big city counterparts. They speak more softly and tread more warily. He had Bukit Mertajam written all over him. I grew to like him very much. He was conscientious and considerate – making me coffee and Milo whenever I looked thirsty or tired. He treated me with such respect and awe, as if I were the arbiter of all wisdom. Working with him was rather like having an intelligent, charming son on hand and for a man with no sons and no prospect of having sons, it was an added pleasure.

Despite our letter of authority, our progress was very slow. There were interminable delays at all the roadblocks. We still had to queue for petrol and because of a puncture outside Tanjong Malim we were a day behind schedule. As such I was growing wary of being able to perform my task on time. And, since I was growing uneasy about the delays I was also getting increasingly crotchety, scolding both Omar and Nazrin at the slightest provocation.

I say I was crotchety with the two of them but there were occasions when I'd realise, often a little too late, that they were trying their level best to match up to my demands and that it was wrong of me to be so harsh. But being an older man and rather old-fashioned at that, I found it difficult to apologise. Nevertheless, two miles outside Tapah in the midst of a rubber plantation, we were forced to stop the car suddenly to allow Nazrin, never the best of travellers, to be sick.

As he squatted and vomited on the side of the road, speckling the baked-red laterite hard-shoulder with the remains of that morning's *nasi lemak*, I shook my head fondly. I rubbed his back and massaged the nape of his neck, reassuring him as best I could.

"There, there, Nazrin, just relax," I said in a fatherly manner, speaking in colloquial Malay.

"Sorry, Tuan, I'm delaying you. You have much more important things to do than look after me being sick here. I'm useless. I shouldn't have eaten the *nasi lemak*," he muttered sheepishly. There was a note of self-recrimination in his voice and I sensed he was close to tears.

"You are silly, young man. You are not useless. I would never be able to complete this mission without you." Hearing my words he lifted his head. I could see he was still in pain as he looked up at me. Despite the yellow spittle at the corner of his mouth and his discomfort, he smiled wanly. His expression was so full of trust and loyalty I felt enormously buoyed up. For that one moment I really wished he was my son. I wished it so passionately that it felt as if my ribs were about to crack under the strain of my fondness for him.

"Nazrin, just rest. We can spare the time," I added as I squeezed the back of his neck warmly. His vulnerability and apologetic tone was very endearing and I appreciated the delicacy with which he handled himself.

Just then, Omar brought some water in a cup for Nazrin. He had fussed around the car boot almost as soon as he'd brought the car to a halt, emerging a few minutes later, cup-in-hand. He, too, was a thoughtful young man. Being uneducated, however, he was less polished though just as respectful of age and seniority as Nazrin. He passed the cup to Nazrin with his right hand. Omar lowered his eyes as I glanced at him. He evaded my eyes in clear demonstration of the subtle distinction in rank that existed between all of us. Whilst Nazrin was my junior, he was Omar's superior and I was left in doubt as to his awareness of these differences.

I was so engrossed in Nazrin that I failed to notice a dog that emerged from the rubber trees on the far side of the road. The animal, a short black pariah with a white chest, trotted across the road. It was quite impervious to our presence and as it passed by I noticed that there seemed to be a garland at the back of its head – something red, curling, bloody and sausage-like. I grimaced. Dogs! How disgusting, they were such foul, dirty animals. Looking closer, however, I saw that the back of the animal's head had been sliced open – as if with a *parang*, and its brains spilt out like a mass of bloody entrails hanging from a pork butcher's stall. Shielding Nazrin's eyes from the sight – I didn't want him to feel any more unwell – I gestured to Omar to shoo the dog away which he did immediately. I could see a look of disgust on Omar's face and a flash of recognition. The dog's horrific wound had reminded both of us of the violence and bloodshed we thought we had left behind.

With a start I knew it was time to move on and get away. Nazrin must have sensed my apprehension because he lifted his head slightly and asked, "Tuan, What was that?"

"Nothing, nothing," I replied hastily. "Come, young man, we'd better go. Can you manage?" With that I helped him back to the car.

"Omar, I think we will have to make up the time lost," I said firmly from the back of the car. "We are late. We are supposed to be in Georgetown by tomorrow. Nazrin, you must rest now but you must watch the time more carefully. We have serious responsibilities. The nation cannot afford delays." Omar grunted and accelerated whilst Nazrin, sitting at the front alongside the driver, pursed his lips and nodded.

Looking out of the car, I watched as row after row of tall oil palm whipped by. At this speed – we must have been going well over 65 miles per hour – all I could sense was the breaks in between each of the rows, the sudden burst of light and space that punctuated the way. Within minutes the neatly variegated rows gave way to a scrappy combination of rice fields and then shabby *bengkels* and lean-tos dotted with school buses, rusty car chassis and lorry vans. The poverty and ugliness of the landscape reminded me once again of my lateness and the great importance of the messages I was carrying in my briefcase.

"Late, late, late. Nazrin, in future you'd better organise my schedule better. I do not want to keep the Gerakan people waiting just because you've been too *kelam kabut*," I said as the car swished past a Chinese settlement. There were small wooden houses on either side of the road, each adorned with a small bright-red altarpiece from which the morning's incense sticks were still burning. Scruffy, mangy-looking dogs lounged in the open gateways beside the ever-present half-dismembered parked cars. I saw, even from the back of the car, that the road narrowed a hundred yards ahead but that it was still straight and the surface regular. There didn't appear to be any roadblocks or gangs.

Relieved by the emptiness of the road I leant back in my seat. Just then, ahead of us, I caught sight of a woman on a bicycle pulling out from the side of the road. She was dressed in a black *samfu* and wore a large straw hat with a wide brim. Thinking nothing of her I turned away just as the car reached alongside her. As we were passing her, I glanced at her again. She was a middle-aged woman and she was hunched over the bicycle like a woman scraping out the flesh of a coconut. Her shoulders were pushed forward. Ripples of fat pressed against her *samfu*. I could see a damp patch of sweat between her shoulders and under her arms. I grimaced – 'Ugh, a real *Cina apeh*'.

In fact we were almost exactly abreast of her when, as if in slow motion, she, without even looking, turned her bicycle abruptly to the right, directly onto the path of our car. Suddenly the middle-aged woman in a *samfu* became something far worse – was she a saboteur, a rioter?

Shouting to Omar I told him to accelerate and get away. In the confusion that followed I can only recall Nazrin's scream as he covered his face with the newspaper to avoid a shower of broken glass, the vicious thud of the woman's body being smashed against the car before she cracked the front window screen and spun off behind the car like a limp rag. Omar braked immediately before coming to a sudden screeching halt. As he did, my head smacked against the headrest in front of me. Dazed by the impact, I fell back in my seat. My head began to throb immediately. The car was silent for a few seconds before Omar spoke.

"*Alamak*, what have I done, Tuan?"

"Tuan, we've killed her." Nazrin's face emerged from his hands. He was crying.

"You fool," I said, steadying myself. The front of my face was burning now. I felt as if someone had beaten me with a clothes iron.

"Drive on, Omar!" I demanded.

"Tuan, how can I? The woman is injured. I must go and see to her." Ignoring me, he pushed his door open and ran back to where her body was lying. I was too much in pain to shout at him. Instead I pushed my own door open. However, the exertion unleashed a terrible searing pain behind my eyes and I was forced to cradle my head in my hands.

"Omar, how is she?" I called out, when, finally I managed to lift my head up and catch sight of her crumpled body. She was smeared in blood and lying some twenty feet behind the car. Her body was splayed out in a grotesque angle, her fat hips swivelled around in one direction, her legs in another. Turning away from her I saw the shattered Raleigh bicycle had been snapped in two. The front wheel was as badly mangled as the woman. It had been flung some twenty feet in front of the car, where it rested on the dirt alongside the tarmac.

But the pain in my head was too great and I covered my face with my hands. Looking through my fingers, I could see that Omar had taken charge of the situation. He was kneeling over her, trying to talk to her and loosening her black blouse. Nazrin, however, seemed to have lost all sense of where he was. He had wandered off the road and away from the car, the bicycle and the woman. He was sobbing uncontrollably: his face blurred by tears and blood. All of a sudden, Omar stood up, grabbed the woman by her arms and dragged her away from the centre of the road.

I knew I had to stand up and assert myself. It was dangerous for us to waste time. It would only be a matter of minutes before the local people found out what had happened, found out that we had knocked down one of their people.

Trouble, there was bound to be trouble.

With that I remembered I had duties to perform, tasks to execute. I had to get on. 'I am entrusted with important tasks,' I said to myself, repeating the phrase over and over again in the forlorn hope that this would clear the pain in my head. Finally, after what seemed like hours – though it could only have been a matter of minutes – I found that I was able to stand up. However, just at the very moment when I was upright, I felt a wave of nausea sweeping over me, knocking at the back of my knees. Collapsing again, I squatted like a schoolkid and vomited abruptly, coughing up thin mucus-like strands of liquid that dripped from my mouth. Doubling up in pain, it felt as if someone was trying to push durian skins down my throat.

Despite the terrible pain in my head and my stomach I knew I had to assert myself. Damn, I thought, what is this? I can't do anything. I can't stand. I'm the emissary of the Prime Minister: how can I take charge if all I can do is cradle my head in my hands? Befuddled and covered in vomit I tried to see what was going on around me, but the figures had become less and less distinct. Peering at them I felt as if I was a silent observer in a play over which I had no control. The plot was written and ordained, the players carrying out their allotted roles. There was nothing for me to do but watch. I, too, was being carried along by the play, passive and unwilling but carried along nonetheless.

The noise had built up around me and though I wasn't sure who was talking or shouting, many of the voices were Chinese. People seemed to rush to and fro and there was commotion as hurried footsteps melded into voices, some speaking Chinese, others speaking Malay, started arguing. I caught a few words: hospital, *mati*, compensation, *duit,* murder, killers. Words, just erratic words. I could hear them but not their context or flow. The exchange was heated but I was unable to figure out who was saying what and why. It was as if I were an onlooker, distanced from the event around me by a pane of glass through which the noise travelled only intermittently, if at all.

As the words became more heated I looked over at the woman. Her inert body was being tended to by a pair of women. Who was she, I wondered? What was her name? Was she a Mei Ling, a Eu Mee, or a Jackie? Her face was inert. Was she dead?

I looked about again and saw that Omar was standing almost alone now – where was that useless Nazrin when he was needed? – fending off what seemed to be a crowd of Chinese men and women from the nearby *kampung*. They were shouting at him and one of them, a woman in a *samfu*, was beating him with her fists. Was she the mother? Was she wailing, crying? I couldn't see that clearly either. Nothing seemed clear. As I looked I began to lose sense of what had happened.

What was going on? Why were they angry with Omar? The fat woman had brought the trouble on herself. She hadn't indicated, hadn't looked, hadn't even bothered. We were just driving by, with important messages to deliver and meetings to attend to: I was the private emissary of the Government. I was a senior civil servant, a 'Tuan'. Confused and in pain I couldn't tell whether the crowd knew who I was. If the situation continued like this we'd be in danger. Running over a Chinese woman was trouble. We should never have stopped. There were more men approaching the fallen woman and they looked tougher. One was wearing a torn dirty T-shirt. The instant he saw her he started screaming, tearing at his T-shirt in a frenzy. There was air of danger about him – something that reminded me in that brief instant, of Chow Kit and Kampung Baru, of fire bombs, gangs and *parangs*. As soon as I sensed the connection I staggered to my feet. That was enough and I shouted at Omar.

45

"Omar, let's get away before they kill us!"

"Yes, Tuan," he shouted back. Both of us ran to the car, though I stumbled as I did. My head was pounding. It was every man for himself. If I hadn't made it to the car, Omar would've had to leave without me – it was that close. Omar, however, had his own problems. Just as he tried to get away, a woman seized hold of him. She started screaming when he wouldn't stop. Foaming at the mouth like an animal, she refused to let go of him. Finally he slapped her across the face. Stunned by the blow, she released her hold. The harsh crack of the slap silenced the noisy crowd momentarily. It was a brief shocked respite. All of a sudden, the crowd erupted as a wave of hatred coursed through them. Electric and vital, it released its evil force into the crowd, unleashing a wave of violence. Hitting out, they punched and beat Omar relentlessly, striking him in the face, in the stomach and on the back. Luckily for him, he managed to pull himself away and dart off to the car. Shaking with fear and sweating profusely, he clambered into the car and slammed the door after him.

"Go! Go! Start the car!" I screamed in Malay. "Or they'll kill us!"

"Where's Nazrin?" Omar shouted back.

"I don't know? Where the hell is that boy?" The car engine roared with one turn of the ignition key.

"It's too late, we can't wait for him, Omar. Go!" With that command I reached forward from the back seat and released the hand brake myself. Pushing Omar sharply with my hand I forced him to drive off. It was just then, as we were speeding off, gathering momentum that Omar saw him, this boy that had been so swiftly discarded.

"*Alamak*, Nazrin's there," Omar shouted. "He's back there and they're beating him with *parangs*."

"No!" I bellowed into Omar's face. "We cannot stop now. We'll tell the police later."

Driving off, I was briefly aware of having done something terribly wrong, of having omitted to do something – of having failed to match up to an essential part of who I was supposed to be. I, a man of distinction, class and learning, a Grade C civil servant, had failed. Even though I now know I could have done very little, I had sunk, allowed myself to sink, sunk to the depths of the mud and grime at the bottom of the Gombak river along with the rotting dog carcasses, worn-out tires, shit and wooden planks. Despite the impossibility of saving Nazrin from his fate, I had sunk to the level of the crowds in Chow Kit and Kampung Baru. They had hacked each other to pieces because they knew no better, because they had no men amongst them who were leaders. I had allowed myself to fall apart, lose direction, lose face, lose respect in the eyes of those from the lower orders. In short I had lost everything because circumstance had, in part, intervened to make my test of manhood so very difficult, so very trying.

Racing away, inchoate thoughts rushed madly around my head, darting from one unrealised fear to another like a ball bearing in a bagatelle as I asked myself desperate, unanswerable questions. What would the crowd do to Nazrin? Would they hack him to bits? Slit his throat? Disembowel him? Slice his head open and spill his brains out like that pariah dog at Tapah? Would the crowd follow us? Were we safe? Would they hunt us down and kill us, too? Was I … responsible?

Had I, in releasing the handbrake, been responsible for it all, for Nazrin's terrible injuries, his crippled state, my fears, and my disgrace?

I had witnessed my own 'fall': lived through it. I had seen myself at my worst. Nothing I could ever do, would match this failure. Aghast, I lost, at least for a few minutes, all control of my faculties as the darkness and the chaos we had tried to banish from the country forever swept its way through me like the passage of a *pontianak* across its victim. Words and phrases tumbled through my mind, in an uneven, ramshackle surge of fear: cowardice; betrayal; catastrophe; chaos; what would Naimah say; self-destruction; loss of face; Fariza my love; death; promotion; disgust; contempt; endgame. I felt as if all as of Syaitan's demons had enveloped me with their darkness.

I had experienced my own terrible cowardice. There was no one else, save Omar and he was just a driver. Who would believe him against me? I had lost myself – stuttering and half-crying with shame and fear, I lowered my head into my hands. Collapsed all around me were the so-called verities and principles I had talked about so readily, principles that I'd lauded and praised only to shirk them in reality. The courage and truth I liked to believe was an integral part of my personality had evaporated. It had been sham, a sham that I had spent years and thousands of dollars trying to cover up thereafter. However, as the minutes passed and we increased the distance between ourselves and the mob, I began to feel an increasing sense of deliverance. We were safe though now my thoughts began to coalesce around an even greater fear and one that was to grow over the decades – the fear of discovery, exposure and almost certain public humiliation.

After twenty minutes Omar pulled over to the side of the road and stopped. He ignored me as he climbed out of the car, pulled a cigarette out of his shirt pocket and lit it. I could see his hands were still shaking as he inhaled on the cigarette, his lips moving rapidly as they formed words that I could barely hear until I leant across the back seat of the car and opened the passenger door near him.

"We ran like dogs with our tails between our legs. We ran like dogs with our tails between our legs. We ran like dogs ..." Standing there, drawing on his cigarette he repeated the phrase, in Malay, to himself as if horrified by what he'd done and what he'd been a party to.

"Omar," I called out in an attempt to reassert myself, "we must go. We are late."

He looked at me directly – something he'd never done in the past. He was only a driver, after all. His eyes were fiery and red –

burning with contempt. His mouth was curled into a sneer as he repeated the phrase one last time, lingering on the word 'dog'.

"We ran like dogs with our tails between our legs." Throwing the unfinished cigarette to the ground, he leant towards me. Spitting the words out, he repeated the phrase once again, this time with a sly smirk that was suffused with anger.

"We ran like dogs with our tails between our legs."

A New Year's Day Lunch in Jalan Kia Peng

"No, not the 'Queen Anne', Latifah. The real silver."

"Yes, Cik Bainun?" Latifah wrinkled her nose and frowned. Cik Bainun looked at her niece and shook her head – the woman was really awfully plain.

"Allah, don't look at me like that – the silver that's under my bed. It's got to be used some time. If we don't use it for the New Year's Day lunch we'll never use it. It's written in the Koran that it's very bad to have silver and gold which you never use – *haram*, you know?" The older lady wagged her forefinger at her niece. Cik Bainun knew she nagged Latifah far too much – it was her way – but she was fond of the woman and felt sorry for her.

"*Adoi*! Such a sour expression. Just because I ask you to fetch the silver from my bedroom. You young people (Latifah was forty-four), I don't know, you're all so ungrateful nowadays – *Melayu Baru* this, *Melayu Baru* that. It doesn't mean we forget how to behave or our *adat*. Politician, politician." Latifah had already turned around and was walking out of the kitchen when Cik Bainun remembered that there was more that she wanted. "Bring the Noritake dinner service and the damask tablecloths as well." The guttural harsh-sounding vowels of her Mendelling ancestry rasped through her Malay.

"Yes, Cik Bainun," Latifah replied grumpily. She resented the way her usual unhurried day was being ruined by the preparations for the New Year's Day lunch. Her aunt had woken her for the *subuh* prayers at five o'clock and kept her busy chopping vegetables, gutting fish, grinding chillies, stirring the *lauks* and curries ever since. She stormed off. Her heavy flat-footed walk could be heard thumping through the wooden house.

Her aunt, Cik Bainun, was sitting cross-legged on a *mengkuang* mat that had been spread over part of the kitchen floor. She was in her mid-seventies and looked rather like a dried-up Chinese plum: tough and chewy but not without flavour. She had a pronounced lower jaw that had made her look like a monkey in her youth. However, as she had grown older, her face had filled out and her appearance had become less simian and more womanly. Still, when she laughed, which was very often, the size of her mouth, lined with gold fillings, was quite astonishing.

There was a pile of blood red rambutans in front of her. She inspected each of the fruit in turn, as if in a factory line: those that passed her scrutiny were transferred to a second, more ordered pile, the damaged and the insect-ridden tossed into a plastic dustbin. When Latifah was not looking she would squeeze open a fruit and pop the egg-shaped orb into her mouth, depositing the seed surreptitiously under the mound of rejected fruit. Cik Bainun, like all her family, suffered from diabetes and Latifah watched over her aunt's diet. Latifah was quick to scold her aunt if she found she had been eating cakes, mangoes or rambutans. As a result, Cik Bainun had had to employ an elaborate series of games and deceptions or else be deprived of her favourite foods. She chewed on the fruit defiantly, sucking at the sweet, forbidden flesh and thought, 'It's going to be a lovely day'.

Ten minutes later Latifah returned, carrying the silver service.

"Yes, that's it," she said excitedly. "Pass the tray so that Cik Bainun (she always referred to herself in the third person) can have a look at it. Oh, but it needs a polish. Call Fuad and tell him to polish it up nicely. Polish first, lay the table second, then mow the badminton court lawn. Lay the table with the Noritake set, don't forget, uh?" She traced the finely engraved words on the centre of the tray as she spoke and thought of her late husband, Raja Zulkarnain, for whom the tray had been a retirement present: 'To the Director-General on his retirement, from the grateful staff of the Ministry of Transport, March 31st, 1974'. She tried not to think of her husband, (she had called him Zul) in the mornings because the memories would crowd into her thoughts and leave her almost paralysed with grief for the rest of the day. He had died only eighteen months before and the memories were still too fresh and sensitive to be touched on without causing pain. She handed the tray back to Latifah, wiped her face with her *selendang* and consoled herself with a rambutan.

For nearly forty years now Raja Zulkarnain's family and friends, or rather the late Raja Zulkarnain's family and friends, had gathered at his residence off the tree-lined Jalan Kia Peng, in order to herald in the New Year with a large lunch-party. He had been the eldest son of one of the wealthiest of Selangor's Territorial Chiefs, Raja Aziz, the Dato' of Kajang who had had the foresight (a fact that the family were to hold out as an example of their greater cunning and intelligence: 'We're not ordinary Bumiputras, you know – we're clever') to stake a claim to the swamps of Sungei Besi long before the advent of the mining engineer and the gravel pump. Despite their princely status they were only very distantly related to the Sultan and that by marriage. There was a story, however, about a claim to the throne of a small Mendelling principality not far from the Sumatran town of Temiang, the exact name of which always seemed to escape their recall. It was a claim that was alluded to all the more readily as the ladies of the family replaced their brass jewellery with silver and then gold.

Despite his distinguished antecedents, Raja Zulkarnain would have been a forgotten relic of feudal days (waxed moustache and all) living in a shabby mansion somewhere in Klang and mumbling about his ancestral *teromba* had he not been the fortunate beneficiary of the enlightened colonial practice of the time. At the tender age of thirteen he was selected for entry to the Malay College. His five years at that august institution had left him with an English accent as plummy as Noel Coward and a propensity to declaim passages from *Twelfth Night* (his Orsino in the 1924 school production had been highly commended). Understandably perhaps, his spoken

Malay was never to recover from the onslaught of the Anglo-Saxon world. After Malay College he was sent to the London University to read Geography (predominantly concerned with those areas of the globe that were, at the time at least, coloured red). He returned to a glittering career, becoming one of the first Malays to rise up through the ranks of the hallowed Malayan Civil Service, crowning his distinguished career with a stint as Director-General of the Ministry of Transport – a fact that was said to account for his collection of Ferraris and Aston Martins and his biannual trips abroad to parts of the world where the laws of banking secrecy were said to be as stringent as his iron-fisted control of transport licences had once been.

However, he had been made a 'Tan Sri' only the year before his death. Such was his character that he refused to use the title, claiming to have been slighted by the very tardiness of its award – "I am a Raja first, a prince – what is this 'Datuk, Datuk, Tan Sri, Tan Sri' to me? If they had given me the title when I fully deserved it I would have been proud of it, but they throw it out to me like scrap meat for the dogs! Bah!" He was not known for his humility and this streak of arrogance had, unfortunately, been inherited by his children, though it was a trait they endeavoured to mask except, of course, when they were amongst themselves.

So it was with a sense of honouring a tradition of considerable standing that the family reassembled at the house that New Year's Day. Tradition, *adat* and custom were the very oxygen of their lives and the grown-up children (though not their spouses) thought nothing of their dutiful trek to Jalan Kia Peng. It was not a religious occasion, nor a family one – none of the family celebrated their birthdays in January. It was a gathering sanctioned solely by habit. But if the truth be told, the late Zul had once attended, when studying in England, the New Year's Day lunch of a university friend and having enjoyed the casual, rather louche meal, had decided as he always did (without discussing the matter with Cik Bainun) to introduce the gathering into his family life as soon as the opportunity arose.

Thus it became, along with his solar topee (purchased at the 'Army and Navy' on The Strand), his MCS chortle, his subscriptions to *Country Life* and *Field*, an aspect of his character and personality that his children had taken to be a true sign of his aristocratic bearing, never for once sensing that what they took to be signs of his nobility were no more than affectations of a world long discredited. People wondered how Cik Bainun could have lived with such an affected prig and one or two had tried to needle her into a confession. Cik Bainun was wise to them: she kept her own counsel. In private, she was more critical of him than she made out in public. Nevertheless she had renewed the magazine subscriptions only the week before even though nobody in the family cared to read about the performance of Purdey's latest high velocity rifles.

She had conducted herself with considerable restraint at her husband's funeral, earning a lot of respect from among the princesses and ladies of the Istana. She had appeared small and frail alongside the catafalque and many of the mourners had thought she would not survive the grief. 'No way she'll stand the loss', 'she's so tiny – sure she'll die within a month', they had said. But they had all underestimated her resources. She emerged from mourning even more crumpled and bent-over but imbued with a strange passion to make the most of the days left to her. Within weeks she had departed for Mecca, dragging along her none-too-willing architect son, Kam. They returned weighed down with gallons of holy water. Kam complained bitterly about having to carry the water but she ignored him. Thereafter, she made twice weekly visits to her husband's grave at the Royal Burial Grounds in Klang, sprinkling the precious water over the grave. When her eldest daughter Mahani had suggested that the New Year's Day lunch be cancelled, she had been so scathing in her reply that the matter had never been raised again.

In the days of Zul's government service the house had seen the comings and goings of petitioners, licence-seekers, small-time Chinese businessmen and UMNO politicians: men who had waited patiently on his verandah for hours on end, accompanied sometimes by their families, knowing that in a simple flick of the wrist, a licence, a taxi licence, a lorry licence could be granted that would lift them up from the uncertainty that clung to their lives.

On his retirement from the civil service Zul had entered the more rarefied world of business. He was appointed Chairman of the Board of McMurtie Estates Berhad, discovering a hitherto unexpected facility in the art of holding board meetings, for which his standard motto was 'No agenda can possibly last more than half an hour'. He was a popular chairman. The house filled with more distinguished visitors: Chinese tycoons accompanied by gun-toting bodyguards, bankers, Malay princes and prominent politicians of all races, a roster of friends and acquaintances who were soon included as guests at the family's New Year's Day lunch. Cik Bainun had preferred the licence-seekers to the businessmen since there was no doubt as to their relative status vis-à-vis the family: they were supplicants and therefore inferior. With the businessmen such matters were far less clear. Civil servants, for example, had their defining rank and position, whether it be Grade H, I, J or Superscale A, B, C, D, E, F or G. Businessmen were indistinguishable. Therefore they all merited equal treatment – a continuous headache for a woman who was expected to entertain them all with her best Noritake and silver.

There was a time then, in the early seventies, when the lunch had become the invitation for New Year's Day as much for the company as for Cik Bainun's food, which Syed Jaffar Albar, 'The Lion of UMNO', had called the greatest cooking outside of Johore – quite a compliment for a Johorean. Tun Razak had come back year after year just to eat her *laksa assam* (she also knew exactly how he liked his Horlicks), Tun Sambanthan for her steaming *teh tarik* and Tun Tan Siew Sin for her deep fried *popiah*. It was even said that much of the NEP had been thought up over her *laksa assam*. She remembered the time a troop of long-eared Sarawakian politicians (led, or so she thought, by Tun Temenggong Jugah) had descended on the house carrying jars of fermented rice wine. They had passed the jars around for everyone to try and Kam had drunk so much that he had been violently sick all over Latifah's toilet.

All that was left of those days, she liked to think, was herself – now a little hard of hearing, thirty seven cats (most of which appeared to have had their tails broken at birth) and her unmarried middle-aged 'niece', Latifah, whose actual relationship to the family was never truly determined. She cooked, cleaned, polished and scrubbed from dawn to dusk, certain of one thing alone – that the monotony of her life was alleviated by her association with Raja Zulkarnain.

As Zul grew older the house, too, had grown quieter, the noise and clamour of visitors subsiding and then totally disappearing when he relinquished the last of his corporate appointments – much to the relief of the Belgian Ambassador who lived next door. The street returned to its look of quiet sobriety and decorum that was its true persona: unrushed, sheltered by swaying raintrees and bamboo groves. But the calm was deceptive and short-lived. Within a few years the house, once so busy, had become a rare, silent redoubt amidst the nocturnal roar of cars arriving at one of the many discotheques and nightclubs that sprang up along the road. By day the awful noise was matched by the growl of the developers' bulldozers.

What had once been a quiet haven of houses and mansions (the Lokes' pink residence was nothing short of a mansion), ornamental gardens, lawns, badminton and tennis courts studded with parterres, tembusus, mimosas and raintrees had given way to the raucous growl of concrete mixers, churned up red earth and fierce-looking Javanese labourers. Still, as long as the redoubtable Zul was still alive it was impossible that the house should be sold and the garden torn up. He had thrown such a fit at the last estate agent who had the temerity to approach him, chasing the man off his property with a pitch fork that even the city's most insistent agents had drawn the line at No. 17 Jalan Kia Peng.

The family home had become her husband's passion and she guarded the house with extreme care, directing its maintenance with a scrupulous eye. It was a large sprawling wooden structure set on nearly two acres, with termites in every beam and sinking foundations. She had treated and re-treated the timbers but no amount of effort seemed to be able to halt the destruction wrought by the white ants and termites. For a full forty years she had lain in bed at night listening to the steady crackle of insects at work. The house had been constructed on low stilts and visitors reached the large open drawing room by climbing a series of steps inlaid with colourful 'Nonya' tiles Zul had bought when stationed in Malacca. The furniture inside the house was eclectic, reflecting the owner's particular passions during his more active years – there were the tiger skins and elephant's feet of his hunting days, the heavy rosewood furniture of his Malacca days, countless glass cases exhibiting gifts and awards that seemed to have attracted dust notwithstanding their airtight containers.

Zul had never been a man to throw anything away and the house benefited from this because it was stamped indelibly with his character – medals, framed pictures, a portrait by Hussein Enas and water colours crowding out all the surfaces, surfaces which his wife wiped and polished with a fanatical dedication.

For each of his three children then, the house was as suffused with memories as the *santan*-scented *kuih lapis* his wife steamed every year for Hari Raya. For Mahani, the eldest daughter, a 'Datuk' in her own right and the Director of the University Hospital, the house (or rather the garden) had been the scene of her first French kiss. This had taken place decades before – after a New Year's Day lunch as it happened. It was hard to imagine that the dignified and business-like fifty-five year old who always wore her hair in a snail-shaped bun was once a wisp of a girl with all the grace and delicacy of a mousedeer. Din, her second cousin, had been the daring kisser (going on to surprise the family by becoming the most devout of religious teachers). He had lured her behind the chicken coop at the back of the garden, grabbed her hands and placed his mouth over hers. She had been shocked and pleased – he was older, wore drainpipes and looked a lot like Cliff Richard. But the force of his embrace had left her shaking.

Mahani was married with four grown-up children, three grandchildren and one erring husband whose latest misdemeanour had been the acquisition of a second wife – 'to save me from committing *zina*', as he put it. She liked to relive her little encounter with Din: if only because it blotted out the awfulness of the present. It made her feel young, invigorated and desired again. She plucked flowers and crunched the sweet-smelling pandan leaves in her fingers as she thought about her little secret, relishing the almost girlish embarrassment she still felt over the kiss and his lizard-like tongue darting into her mouth. At the time it had seemed the height of sinfulness and wicked beyond belief: 'if only,' she thought, 'I had known better'.

Meriam, the second daughter (also a grandmother), was a more homely woman. She had large plump buttocks, the family jaw, her mother's laugh and the best *kuih seri muka* in all of Shah Alam. She gravitated towards the kitchen where she felt at ease among the smells and cumin stains. She peered into the storeroom, examined the vegetables, pried open the fish gills to check their freshness, tasted the curries and questioned Latifah on the household expenses. Being the least well-off of the family (she was married to a MARA lecturer), she considered it her duty to apply her own very stringent and parsimonious housekeeping principles to her mother's kitchen. What she failed to bestow in material terms she more than compensated – in money saved by re-using the frying oil and not throwing it away, by buying vegetables from the *pasar tani* and using beef shin whenever possible and cooking it for hours on end until it fell off the bone to the touch.

A New Year's Day Lunch in Jalan Kia Peng

Finally there was the apple of Cik Bainun's eye, her Kam. He was her youngest child and only boy. Like all only sons, he was horribly spoiled and conceited. His self-absorption was made worse by his jaunty golf-tanned exterior and high pitched nasal voice. He was as thin as his sister Meriam was fat and laughed at her penny-pinching.

Whilst he laughed at Meriam endlessly – she was the 'Ratu Cheap Sale' – Mahani was a different matter. People often referred to him as Datuk Mahani's brother. The mere mention of her name was enough to reduce him to a state of green-eyed jealousy. In private, he compared their respective newspaper coverage, counting the column inches (and photographs) with all the feverishness of an ambitious journalist. It was not that he was unsuccessful. Far from it. He detested the thought that people might think less of him the more they thought of Mahani. He was the of one of the city's most prominent architects and was well known for his distinctive trademark – deeply-pitched Minangkabau roofs. Even so, he had yet to be anointed a 'Datuk'.

He had married Chew Mei Mei, a Chinese girl, breaking his mother's heart in the process. At the time, the marriage seemed set to be a catastrophe: his mother had wept disconsolately for weeks, mumbling the word *'kafir'* in her dreams. 'Fat Chew', as Mei Mei's father was called, was a follower of Confucius and a devoted eater of pork. He winced to think of his daughter's conversion to Islam: "all *sembahyang, sembahyang* – banging your head on the floor". But the marriage, oiled by the father-in-law's tin-mining fortune, had been a quiet success and Mazlinda, as she was now called, was as welcome in her in-law's houses as Kam was in his. Besides, her father's propensity for mistresses and concubines (he had had five on his deathbed) had prepared the daughter for her own husband's inevitable transgressions.

Raja Zulkarnain's death eighteen months before had freed the three children from the tiresome obligation of being nice to one another. In the past their father's looming presence had been enough to quell any outward display of anger or dislike. Every Sunday lunch they were expected to assemble and converse with one another, notwithstanding their mutual antipathy. The old man had long favoured his eldest daughter, despairing, in turn, of his son's bumptiousness. "He may be my son, Noon, but that doesn't mean I have to like him," he would say. As if to compensate for her husband's favouritism, Cik Bainun, or Noon as he called her, lavished Kam with all her love and attention. Meriam was neglected entirely. She spent her days in the servant's quarters, learning how to cook and clean. As her father commented, "My daughter has learnt how to cook and mix with the lower orders: it was no surprise to me that she married Shahrir – who else would have her?".

A new source of misunderstanding had arisen between Kam and his two sisters. They had heard rumours that Kam wanted to knock down their father's house and build condominiums. Kam knew the sisters would be unwilling. Therefore he had chosen his first target well, mentioning the idea in passing to Meriam's husband Shahrir. Kam had seen Shahrir buying cigarettes one stick at a time and knew it was only a matter of time before the money became too potent for Shahrir. He enticed Shahrir with figures that seemed obscene – enough, Kam had calculated, to settle all his brother-in-law's debts and buy a new terrace house in Subang Jaya's Phase 8. Having mentioned the subject to his perennially hard-up brother-in-law he had repeated the figures every few months or so. As expected, Shahrir told Meriam who quite unexpectedly told Mahani who threw a self-righteous fit – thus upsetting his neatly laid plans.

Kam had dreamed of the idea from the day he first qualified as an architect. He had dreamed continuously of the apartments that he would build on the plot of the land (they transmuted into condominiums sometime in the early eighties), the ratios, the densities and the design: a simple, elegant structure with pitched Minangkabau roofs. Whilst he was sympathetic to his father's conservatism, his dream of building, the overwhelming desire to plan,

A New Year's Day Lunch in Jalan Kia Peng

execute and construct, was so ingrained in his psyche that it was impossible for him to look at the land without envisaging what he, the great Raja Kamarul, could make of the spot. It was with these tantalising thoughts in his mind that he drove to his mother's house. He was determined to win them over.

"It won't be the same," Mei Mei said slowly, half to herself. "It just won't be the same without *your* father. The house, the gardens, Meriam's *rendang*, even the coronation chicken; it'll all be different. Like empty. No Ayah." Kam grunted. Twenty years of marriage had inured him to much of his wife's endless prattling, inured him to the noise but never the content. She continued, her chain of thought unbroken.

"Mak is so strong. I want to cry when I think of how she was when Ayah's body was brought back ... she didn't cry, so brave. She stood all alone and she was so small in that house – she didn't want us to be with her."

"Sabrina, your mother is too sentimental. But she's right about one thing: the house is too big for Mak." There was a note of irritation in his voice now and he rounded the corner in an aggressive manner, cutting so close to the kerbstone that car shook from the jolt. He corrected himself angrily as if blaming his wife for his mistake. In the rear of the car, his teenage daughter Sabrina was hurled across the backseat.

"Father!" But both parents ignored her.

"Kam, I would have been broken if it had been you."

"You, uh, always want to dramatise. We are not a *Drama Minggu Ini* kind of family. Ayah was my father but I don't go on about it. Don't talk about it all the time. You're right though, I must talk to her about the house – it's just too big." Kam, her husband, was not a man of great emotion – in fact, his last mistress but one, 'Jamilah Jamboo' (on account of the firmness of her buttocks), had commented on Kam's determination to meet with her and have sex on the night of his father's death. "That boy," she had said later, shuddering in remembrance, "he's like a grindstone: there's nothing soft, nothing gentle about him. Bang, bang, bang – finish. I don't know why he doesn't go to Chow Kit. Cheaper for him." Unsurprisingly perhaps, 'Jamilah Jamboo' forsook the fierce but clammy embrace of her rich architect lover for a demure Selangor State Assemblyman three times her age whose exaggerated devotion was as extreme as Kam's neglect had once been.

Kam had been deeply shamed by her desertion. Within an hour of hearing of her perfidy he had cancelled all her supplementary credit cards and changed the locks on their love nest in Wisma Stephens. He feared ridicule more than anything else in the world – the kind of ridicule that would ensue when people realised that he had been jettisoned in favour of a dithering YB old enough to be his father.

From that hour on, he excised 'Jamilah' from his life, acquiring a new mistress whose chief qualification was that she was pencil thin and without any discernible buttocks. It had all been achieved in as perfunctory and clinical a manner as possible, because for Kam, emotions – the messy things that women tried to blackmail him with in the morning – were a hindrance to the art of making buildings that made money that paid for the likes of 'Jamilah Jamboo'.

Cik Bainun was making a final check of the preparations as Kam's car pulled up the driveway. She had just rearranged the flowers and switched the cutlery around (Fuad, the houseboy, had never been able to tell the difference between left and right). Looking up from the dining table she saw Latifah and smiled.

"I want you to wear that nice new *baju kurung* I bought you and put a bow in your hair – you can take one from my dressing table." It was a lovely day and she wanted everybody to be happy. She walked up to the main door, repeating the words in English to herself, as she did – 'a lovely day'. She greeted Kam and Mei with the serenest of smiles.

"*Assalaamualikum.*"

"*Wa'alikumsalaam,*" Cik Bainun replied.

"Mak, you're looking lovelier than ever," he said in English and hugged her. Sabrina bobbed down to kiss her grandmother's hand as Mei kissed her mother-in-law on both cheeks warmly.

"Kam, Mak is an old lady," Cik Bainun replied in Malay. She was touched, nonetheless, by his flattery and flushed.

"Mak, Kam's right, you *are* looking lovely," Mei said.

"You do, Nenek!" Sabrina joined in enthusiastically.

"Doesn't matter. The others are already here, come in, come in. Everyone except Mahmud – Mahani says he's got food poisoning." There was a moment's knowing silence before Kam spoke.

"*Laksa assam*, this year? I'm so hungry."

"Well, there's no *tapai*," she teased, laughingly. Mei looked on and smiled. It still amazed her that her Kam could be so sweet and charming. Sabrina rushed ahead and salaamed each of her aunts and uncles, embracing her elder cousins and kissing their young children. Cik Bainun watched her granddaughter's energetic progress, the way she flicked the hair out of her eyes and twirled the babies up in the air. 'Just like Mahani,' she thought.

As with the year before and the years before that, there was an abundance of food. The conversation, too, was no different from previous years: Meriam complained about her diets – 'they just aren't working' – as she ladled a third helping of rice onto her plate; Kam gorged himself on his mother's *laksa assam*, belched very loudly and then lit up an enormous cigar (to the delight of the young children who loved watching him roll the end of the cigar through the flame of his Dunhill lighter); Mahani, who watched her weight closely, took some *rojak*, skimping on the sweet black sauce and the *sayur lodeh*. Cik Bainun insisted on taking some of the rich *ayam percik* and *ayam kuzi* even though Latifah looked on disapprovingly.

The conversation around the table ebbed and flowed. No one mentioned Mahmud's absence, the house or the 'condos'. As Kam lit up his cigar the conversation seemed to rise to a crescendo; everyone at the dining table, save Cik Bainun, seemed to have something to say. Mahani was telling her admiring nieces about the hospital, "It's hard work – like running a hotel where every guest has a complaint." Mahani's accent was the most English of all the children.

Not one to be outdone, Kam started talking about his latest project as Sabrina, at the far end of the table, mimicked the rock star Ella's singing style, 'Like this, ah, Ciiiintaaaaaarghhh' and one of the babies – Cik Bainun's great-grandchild (who happened to be teething) – started wailing.

Cik Bainun sat at the head of the table, her face wreathed in smiles. She wasn't listening to any one particular conversation – as a mother, she had already heard everything her brood had to say. But rather, she was listening to the noise, to the disordered rush of conversation, children's cries and scraping chairs. And, like a bather on an empty beach during the monsoon, she was enveloped in the all-encompassing roar of the ocean and the elements. Lost in the fullness of the sounds surrounding her, oblivious to the particular and the detailed.

"Take this house," Kam said expansively, throwing his arms out in a wide arc. "Just imagine the potential." Mahani who was talking to Meriam's daughter Zarina, ignored his comment studiously.

"A job is a job. Being a doctor is more of a calling: you don't do it for the money – you do it for the love of it." She was a role model to her nieces and the one that they came to with their problems.

"How's the baby? Has he still got colic?"

"It's been terrible, Auntie Mahani. I've been awake every night for the past week – every time I put him down he cries and the husband refuses to get up."

"… a beautiful shimmering block topped by with a Minangkabau roof set amidst landscaped gardens …"

"– says he has work to do. As if I don't! I fell asleep at the office the other day and started snoring. That and the housework, his family are always coming to stay …"

"... an Eden in the city ..."

"Don't you have a Filipino maid?"

"Yes, but she's so new I've got to show her everything."

"... a dignified row of imperial palms with bougainvillea hanging from every balcony; lanais lined with black slate and shuttered windows ..."

"... yesterday she put washing powder down the toilet and it foamed over every time we flushed it."

"You poor thing."

"Auntie Mahani, I wish I was more like you. You make it sound so easy."

"... two acres of land at thirty units per acre with a swimming pool and a squash court thrown in ..."

"Easy? It's not easy, *sayang*. There are sacrifices." Mahani paused, not wanting to continue.

"Price the condos at four hundred thousand each and our profit margin is at least fifty per cent. That's the future – condo-living: all the facilities, security with none of the hassles. No snakes, no mosquitoes, no *cicaks*, Mak. So, Mak, what do you think?" Kam spoke in Malay, smiling at his mother. But Mahani interjected before Cik Bainun could reply.

"Yes, Kam, kick your mother out of the only house she has known all her life so that you can build the condominiums of your dreams," Mahani said sarcastically. She had spoken in Malay, the language of all their arguments. Everyone else fell silent. Shahrir, Meriam's husband, lowered his face into his coffee. Cik Bainun awoke from her reverie suddenly – the waters had receded: all around her there were rocks.

"Put your mother in a condo with all the mistresses and tarts!" she added aggressively.

Kam smirked and replied, "That maybe what Mahmud has done with his second wife, Kak. I wouldn't do that to my mother."

"*Astagfirullah*, my brother? Is this what it's come to? And who was keeping 'Jamilah Jamboo' in Wisma Stephens until she ran off with the fat YB?" Brother and sister stared at each other in silent fury. But it was too much for Cik Bainun who called out angrily.

"Silence! Silence! I will not have this kind of talk at my table. Please, for your late father's sake."

"I'm sorry, Mak, but you heard her?"

"Both of you, apologise!"

"No!"

"Apologise, please!" There were tears in her eyes.

"I'm sorry, Kak."

"I'm sorry, Kam." But there was still enough malice in both their hearts to poison all the inhabitants of the putative condominium project.

"I think it's time the children had their badminton game," Cik Bainun said. Saddened, she left the table and walked out onto the verandah, her heart heavy with foreboding. She had been able to stop them today. But she wasn't going to be around in the future.

She sat down on the cane armchair as if suddenly she had been made aware of her own powerlessness. She hugged herself. Zul was gone: his calming presence and authority all gone. She was alone – with no Zul to fend for her. She looked out across the verandah. There were memories of Zul all around her, pressing against her like gusts of warm rain-soaked winds. She wanted to be strong and willed herself not to cry – not to succumb on this, his favourite day of the year.

An electric-blue kingfisher was perched on the raintree opposite the verandah. The bird twitched irritably. Even the birds, she thought, were distressed. She looked away as the powerful gusts enveloped her. All she could think of was the hopelessness of the days that were left to her. Days and nights that would be filled with the petty squabbles of her own children. The ugly thoughts crowded in on her and she sobbed quietly on the verandah while the family prepared for the badminton match.

The match was another of the New Year's Day rituals. Each year the younger generation challenged the older to badminton. For the past two years, the children had actually won and everyone enjoyed the ramshackle match. The year before, there had been fifteen players on the court: the numbers were augmented by Cik Bainun's great-grandchildren. There had not been enough badminton racquets to go around and her '*cit-cit*' had had to make do with tiny hockey sticks, tennis and squash racquets as well as one small plastic spade.

As the children filed onto the court and knocked the shuttlecock backwards and forwards over the net Cik Bainun slowly regained her composure. She dabbed her eyes with her handkerchief and watched as Sabrina darted from side to side, tumbling onto the ground with her nephews and nieces in a good-humoured maul.

Finally Kam, Meriam, Shahrir and Mahani emerged onto the court. Kam had a devilish slam that he had employed to good effect over the years; Shahrir was a drop-shot specialist; Mahani, a solid defensive player; and Meriam, an unmoving presence in the middle of the court. The sisters were the 'Sidek Brothers' in family parlance and Kam, 'Ardy the Indonesian'. Nobody had bothered to think of a name for Shahrir. When Kam was in a good mood, which he wasn't this year, he would give a running commentary on the game in heavily accented Indonesian Malay – "*Sekarang saudara Ardy menunggu serbis.*" Even Latifah had laughed.

Mahani and Kam observed a frosty silence, ignoring one another on the court. When Kam miss-hit the shuttlecock, making it land at his sister's feet, she ignored it and then trod on it just as he was about to bend down and pick it up. Meriam and Shahrir exchanged embarrassed glances: their cramped terrace house was more welcome than 'World War Three' on the courts.

"Everyone ready?" Sabrina and her cousin Zarina called out in unison.

"Yes," her father replied. "Get on with it."

"No, Uncle Kam," Zarina replied firmly. "We must repeat the rules – so no cheating or disagreeing." Kam grunted and Mahani swung her racquet through a wide arc before bringing it down in a mock smash. There was a curious half-smile on her face. Zarina continued.

"Your court extends as far as the nangka trees at the back, the bougainvillea on the left and the path on the right. Auntie Mei is the line judge: all her decisions are final. Our court extends to the right as far as the flowers in front of the house and on the left as far as the path. The driveway is the backside of the court (Sabrina giggled as Zarina frowned – "It's not funny, Sabrina!"). If a shuttlecock is hit into the raintree that point shall be taken again."

But another of the cousins objected. "No, they always hit it into the tree: that's unfair."

Kam scowled. "Oh, shut up and let's play."

"We'll serve first then."

"Just get on with it, Zarina."

"One–love," the youngsters chanted in unison as Zarina's drop shot of a serve fell beside Mahani, unnoticed.

"I wasn't ready!"

"Sorry, Auntie Mahani, Uncle Kam said to get on with it." Mahani narrowed her eyes angrily and pulled up her sleeves.

Zarina served once again, though this time the service was retrieved by Kam who knocked it back with a sharp tap. Sabrina intercepted the shot and lobbed it high over Uncle Shahrir.

"Duck," Meriam shouted, "I'll get it." And she did with a fierce smash that hit one of her grandchildren on the head.

"Hah," she cried, not noticing the injury. "Love–one. Our serve." And so the game progressed with both sides notching up points as Mahani and Kam continued to ignore each other. As the game reached 13–13, both sides started taking things more seriously – Meriam took off her earrings and Mahani hitched up her *baju kurung*.

A New Year's Day Lunch in Jalan Kia Peng

Shahrir served a deft little shot that had Sabrina stretching to return it. "Damn." She had pushed the shuttlecock high above the net and her father jumped up to smash the shuttlecock.

"14–13." This time Meriam served and her son-in-law smashed the shuttlecock back across the net. Embarrassed by her puny service she lumbered up to the shot.

"*Alamak*, is it an elephant?" Kam said in Malay under his breath as his sister thundered by. She rammed the shot back vigorously.

"*Celaka!*" But the shot had not been firm enough to win the point and Sabrina had returned it with a drive straight down the middle of the court, right between her father and Mahani. Since neither was talking to the other they rushed for the shot and crashed into one another with a dull thud and fell to the ground. Miraculously the shot was returned: the point and the game won.

Mahani was sitting on top of her brother and laughing. Kam looked up and started laughing. As the adversaries laughed, everyone else joined in, partly out of relief and partly because of the humour of the moment. From the balcony Cik Bainun clapped her hands excitedly.

"Better than the Thomas Cup, eh, Latifah?" she said.

The next game was an anticlimax as the youngsters took the lead and never lost their serve, winning 15–3.

"Daddy, you're too old-*lah*," Sabrina said good-humouredly. "Only good for one game." The third and final game was a more tense affair – the little ones with the squash and tennis racquets were told to sit down. The youngsters opened with the service but soon lost it when Sabrina hit the shuttlecock into the net at 4–love. The parents served carefully and smashed each of the returns to level the score.

"Too old, your father?" Meriam asked rhetorically. Kam was sweating profusely. The damp patches under his arms had expanded to reach the one in the middle of his chest as well as the one at the small of the back.

When the score reached 8–8, Mahani loosened her hair bun, Meriam belched and Shahrir continued trying to look unobtrusive.

The game swung back to the youngsters as Kam's smashes grew a little inaccurate and Meriam was unable to run for shots that were more than a stretch away. At 12–8, Mahani spoke out angrily.

"Come on-*lah*, Meriam, we can't let them win!" Mahani was exasperated by her sister's inability to move.

"Yes, Meriam, move your fat bottom!" Kam added. "No need to diet, just run."

"You think it's easy. I'm a grandmother-*lah*, you know?"

"So's Mahani. Just move those fat thighs." Meriam's daughters giggled as their uncle and aunt teased their mother. They were sure of victory now. But in their overconfidence they lost their concentration and the parents were able to claw back four vital points to level the score. As Mahani or Kam smashed each of the winning shots, all four of the parents shouted out excitedly.

"Yeh!" By this time Kam was drenched in sweat. His hair was dripping. Sabrina and her cousins were swearing at each other. They dearly wanted to extend their winning streak.

At 13–12, Shahrir missed an easy dropshot and the service passed back to the youngsters.

"This isn't *sepak takraw*. Hit the shuttlecock with your racquet, not your kneecap," Kam said dismissively. The shuttlecock had hit him on the knee. But the youngsters fluffed both their services (Sabrina was almost in tears). Cik Bainun shook her head in sympathy; they'd been so close.

Meriam served at 13–12. Her nephew-in-law returned the shot. Shahrir rushed up to the net and slammed the shuttlecock into the top of the net, where it was caught for a brief second before toppling onto the opposing side.

"Whoa!" he shouted, raising his fist in the air. Cik Bainun looked on in surprise. She had never seen him look so excited. Mahani and Meriam screamed in delight and Kam patted him on the back.

"Great stuff," Kam added. Mahani served for the match. A long, painfully drawn-out rally ensued as the two sides returned the shuttlecock with graceful shots that swept deep into both courts. By now everybody, including Latifah and Fuad, the houseboy, was gathered around the court, gasping each time the shuttlecock was hit, their heads swivelling from side to side.

Sabrina was the first to falter. She miss-hit her father's attacking shot. The shuttlecock flew up into the air directly above Meriam's head. It was an easy smash and everyone knew it – unfortunately Meriam had missed many of the smashes she attempted. Nonetheless she swallowed deeply and took a step back. Jumping up as best as she could, she smashed the shuttlecock with such ferocity that it crashed to the ground on the opposite side of the net.

Mahani threw her badminton racquet up into the air and hugged her sister, screaming "We won, we won." Meriam smiled exuberantly. Extricating herself from Mahani's embrace, she ran up to Shahrir. They hugged and laughed. Meanwhile, Kam looked at Mahani, tilted his head to one side as if to say, 'I'm sorry, let's be friends'. Cik Bainun watched as they walked up to one another and hugged. She felt the tears in her eyes and pulled at the handkerchief that she kept in her sleeve. At last, she thought, we are one again, just as Zul would have wanted.

She remained on the verandah as the players trooped back into the house, calling for cold drinks. Sabrina and her cousins sulked, storming off to the kitchens. Though Cik Bainun was sorry for her grandchildren she was relieved that their parents had won and that the unpleasantness of lunch had been overcome. Maybe it was possible for Mahani and Kam to live together – a bit more tolerance and thought would teach them both the importance of compromise. Kam was a forgiving and understanding boy. If only Mahani wasn't so headstrong. She knew that Kam would never touch the house – that it was all talk, silly talk. He was an architect! Of course, he was going to talk about building things all the time but she knew that he loved the house as much as her and that he wanted to keep it just the way it was – in memory of Zul. He was a fine boy. She sighed and looked off into the distance. Up in the raintree overlooking the badminton court, the kingfisher hopped from branch to branch. She watched as the bird preened itself, displaying sudden flashes of colour. This was the loveliest garden in the city. Where else could they play badminton? At the Lake Gardens? In Petaling Jaya? This was their home. She felt at peace once again – it had been a lovely day.

Just then she heard Kam's voice. He was speaking in Malay. He whispered the words angrily.

"There's no such thing as a free lunch, Shahrir (he seemed to be speaking through his teeth). I've paid you already. You'd better work on your fat wife. Get her to persuade Mahani or I'll tell her about your problem with the English lecturer – abortion, wasn't it? Mak will have fallen for that little charade outside. She'll do whatever I want. Damn this house. I have to knock it down within six months and get building by the end of the year at the latest. Building costs are going up every week. I can't afford to hang around. I'm not putting up with another of these bloody lunches again … no sir."

The Inheritance

"A good death, like a good rain, really brings the toads out of hiding," Mahmud drawled under his breath. He had a throaty, hoarse voice, the timbre of which seemed yellowed with nicotine.

"*Yeh-geh?*" his dim-witted brother-in-law, Ahmad, asked. Mahmud, by way of contrast, was well known for his mischievous sense of humour – something that had made him welcome in many of the more select KL homes and princely residences, despite his remarkable ugliness and bad dress sense. *Selekeh* in all things, he was small and dark with a badly pock-marked face and a chin so weak it seemed to rest halfway down his neck. Nonetheless Mahmud had been the most popular of Usman Khalid's four sons-in-law: the most popular but not necessarily the most trusted.

Sitting next to Mahmud in an immaculately starched and uncreased *baju* was his fellow brother-in-law, Tajuddeen. Tajuddeen (no one called him 'Din') was tall and trim. He was the most able and trusted of the sons-in-law. Ability, however, did not equate with personability and Tajuddeen was not popular man. An accountant by training he had left the profession in the mid-'80s in order to steer the deceased man's many companies through the economic squalls of those years. Stern and unflinching in matters of business he applied the same enduring principles of thrift and self-discipline to his private life – much to his family's deep dismay. He was well known for his meanness and Mahmud in particular had had great pleasure recounting a story about how Tajuddeen still wore, and with pride, the same set of Y-fronts that he'd been married in some twenty-two years before.

However, it was a measure of parsimony that was applied to all. Unlike many other wealthy men he really did live simply. Even after all these years when others breakfasted on croissants and cappuccino, Tajuddeen merely indulged in the odd RM1 packet of *nasi lemak. Teh tarik*, he saved for special occasions. Warm water – *air suam* – was his customary drink. His in-laws, being pure-blooded Kelantanese from Tanah Merah and therefore rather full of themselves, looked down on his honest, if uncompromising, ways. They thought him unutterably vulgar and common. Rich men, as far as they were concerned, were supposed to be dashing and debonair or, if not, they were like Mahmud – enormously entertaining. Distinction was accorded those who were lavish and showy. As a result they winced whenever Tajuddeen delivered one of his little homilies on the virtues of Bata shoes and property in Kepong Baru Utama. In some circles such virtues might have been praised and commended. In the family of the late Usman Khalid they were tolerated in public and vilified in private.

"Penang *mamaks*," Mahmud would sneer. "What do you expect? They try so hard they forget they're supposed to be human. The way he has grovelled with Ayah in the past few years. *Alamak*, even you'd be sick to watch it. Of course, even the best laid plans can come to grief …"

That evening, Mahmud, whilst ignoring his stern brother-in-law, maintained his light-hearted commentary as the mourners arrived.

"Ayah would have loved it," he whispered. "Why, even Tengku Kamil's here and he hated Tengku Kamil."

"Really? Is that true, Tajuddeen?" Ahmad asked eagerly, only to be ignored by both brothers-in-law. Instead, Tajuddeen nodded at a recently arrived mourner. Mahmud continued and whilst smiling broadly at the same mourner he replied to Ahmad.

"Loathed him," he pronounced emphatically, lingering on words lovingly for effect, "I bet Tengku Kamil's here to make sure Ayah's truly dead. He never forgave Ayah for getting the Ulu Sepang contract. Spit on the grave, you know?"

"No-*lah*!" Ahmad gasped. Tajuddeen remained silent. He disapproved of such disrespect. Ahmad turned instinctively to his late father-in-law's body laid out in state on the catafalque in front of the three of them. The old man's stern face was all that was exposed by the white calico sheets that had been neatly tied under his prominent jaw – a jaw that had earned him the sobriquet *Pak Monyet* from his enemies.

"You're so naive, Ahmad," Mahmud continued. "Nothing else would have prised him away from his polo ponies. Oh, I need a cigarette. 'Give me my poison!' is what I say. All this mourning is making my throat dry. After all, I have to figure out how to spend the wife's inheritance. Four daughters-eh? No sons-uh? Sure-uh? (poking Tajuddeen in the ribs as he spoke) Big responsibilities or is it big money? You'll learn, Ahmad, you'll learn. See you later."

Mahmud smirked. He cleared his throat with a noisy flourish before straightening his overlong and crumpled *sarung*. Tajuddeen frowned as Mahmud walked off. Ahmad shook his head as he watched his brother-in-law cross the sitting room floor. However, Tajuddeen turned away, his jaw tightly clenched with irritation. Mahmud was dispensing greetings like a politician: salaaming quickly and firmly, smiling benignly all the while. He noticed how Mahmud moved through the room – plotting his course by the prominent Tan Sris and Datuks, stopping for a few seconds at each to express heartfelt thanks and receive the warmest of condolences. With Tengku Kamil, Mahmud paused for a good minute, before proceeding on to the hallway and out of the front door.

Cars were doubled-parked along the driveway. A small group of chauffeurs leant against the children's swing on the front lawn. Smoking clove cigarettes, they joked and laughed whilst exchanging stories about their bosses. They fell silent as Mahmud's wizened figure approached them. Almost immediately, the men who had been leaning against the swing stood up, brushing out the creases in their trousers. Mahmud stopped two feet away from the group. To an onlooker, it was as if he had chosen deliberately to stand slightly apart from the men so that the great difference in height should not be too pronounced. Having established his authority he demanded a cigarette, speaking in the sing-song Kelantanese Malay of his youth that he now saved for the servants.

"Give me one! No-*lah*, not the Gudang Garam. Wah, you can afford Dunhill? Who's your boss? Tan Sri. That's why, mmph! Too much overtime. Light? Call me if you see an outstation taxi from Tanjong Malim! Don't forget! There's twenty dollars for the one who tells me first."

Having lit the cigarette he sauntered off. There was a slight bounce in his step, an unfamiliar lightness as he paced across the soft cow grass of his father-in-law's front lawn and returned to the house. Night was falling and the men from the *surau* were expected at any moment for the prayers. Mahmud stood in a pool of light by the porch and inhaled deeply on the cigarette. As the men chanted quietly within the house he smiled to himself. Funerals, he loved funerals. There was always the chance of a little drama, a little uncertainty. Funerals, funerals: dead men and their wives. Sniggering to himself he exhaled, forming a neat ring of cigarette smoke that rose languidly into the darkness.

Back in the house Tajuddeen fingered the thick wedge of cash (twenty dollar notes) in the pocket of his *baju*. He touched the notes with assurance. He knew that he alone among the brothers-in-law would have had the presence of mind to arrange money for the men from the *surau*. Nonetheless, Mahmud's sly insinuations had unsettled him. However, he had learnt not to rise to the bait. He knew that the other three – Mahmud included – were hopeless. His father-in-law had been forced to bail the others out time and again as they failed at one venture after another. He alone had excelled. He alone had been dutiful and correct in all things – taking the mother-in-law on her *umrahs* over the years, waiting by the father's hospital bed during his final, almost interminable stint in the ICU. No. There was no one else. He felt sure his father-in-law recognised his superiority. Four daughters and no sons: four sons-in-law but only one man. Confident in his position he raised his head up and looked about him, bathing in the glorious incompetence and mediocrity of his in-laws.

Meanwhile Mahmud entered the house again through the hallway. Checking the grandfather clock he saw that there were still another fifteen minutes until *waktu maghrib*. He tipped the cigarette ash carelessly into the ashtray and strode into the kitchen where he stood and surveyed the preparations – the *lauks*, the fried chicken, the freshwater prawns and the bowls of *acar*. Scanning the food he caught sight of the new Indonesian maid, Ani. She was standing with her back to him. The back of her neck was fair. Her body was nicely-proportioned – shapely even, with generous buttocks. Just as he was about to place his hands on the tempting rump she turned around. He smiled at her knowingly as she did, stubbed his cigarette out on a coffee saucer and then walked back into the hallway. Ani could wait till later, he was more interested in bigger game.

As he walked out of the kitchen he bumped into Tajuddeen who had decided to come to the front of the house in order to greet the men from the *surau*. Standing alongside Mahmud, Tajuddeen noticed the full ashtray. His late father-in-law had not been a stickler for order. Ignoring Mahmud very pointedly, he picked up the ashtray and marched into the kitchen where he found a slightly flustered Ani.

"This is not to happen again, do you understand? I will not stand for it." His words were terse but just loud enough for Mahmud to hear. She nodded mutely. He disliked Indonesians as a rule. All the maids in his house were Filipinos. They didn't run away or rather they couldn't run away and get married. He'd tried explaining once to his mother-in-law but she'd refused to see sense. She'd see sense soon enough, he thought to himself and so would Mahmud.

Tajuddeen stepped out into the hallway again. He saw that his mother-in-law was about to descend from her bedroom. All four of the daughters were in attendance. The women had obviously been crying together. He caught his wife Aishah's eye and stepped aside, allowing the women to pass in a sad but united group. However, Mahmud failed to do so and his mother-in-law saw him. She grabbed hold of Mahmud and hugged him with all her strength.

"Mahmud," she wailed in Malay, "Ayah is dead. You must look after us. You are my only son. Ayah is dead!"

"Mak, you're going to have to do your ablutions again," Aishah remarked softly as she tried to pull her mother away.

"It's alright, Mak," Mahmud replied simply. "Go and sit down, the men will be here soon." With that he eased her away from him and directed her, gently, towards his wife, Aniza.

"Ayah!" she screamed. "Why have you left me?" Covering her face with her *selendang*, she sobbed bitterly before being guided and half-carried into the study where there was a guest bathroom. Mahmud wiped his face with his hand. Despite the emotional outburst he felt somewhat elated. Tajuddeen turned and looked away.

Ten minutes later, after the old lady had completed her ablutions for the second time, the women made their way across the living room to a specially cordoned-off area. There, the five of them sat down with Aishah, Tajuddeen's wife and the eldest, to the right of his mother-in-law and Aniza, Mahmud's wife, to the left. Tajuddeen watched how Aishah, using the corner of her own *selendang*, wiped her mother's face. She was a good daughter, his wife. Sitting quietly they mouthed prayers as they tried not to look at their late father's body resting on the catafalque.

Tajuddeen thought that the five of them in their mourning constituted a distinguished group: all in white, their eyes red with tears. The circumstances obscured for once the fact that they were not an attractive group of women. Each of the four girls had inherited their father's pronounced lower jaw and shallow fish-like eyes. The combination in the old man had looked distinguished. Unfortunately for the girls it had made them look ungainly and stupid. However Tajuddeen, for once, was too engrossed in his own thoughts to think of the physical unattractiveness of his in-laws. All he could think of was the years he'd spent biting his tongue, ignoring their snide comments, turning a blind eye to their inanities and smiling on their feeble achievements.

Finally, it was all worthwhile. He had waited a long time – twenty-two years to be exact – for this moment, waiting as silently as a great cat in the *belukar*. He had plotted patiently, acquiring company directorships, cars, land and greater responsibility whilst the other sons-in-law had failed and moved on. Countless millions and only four daughters. Breathing in deeply, he beamed with pride.

Just then, he heard a car pull up in the driveway. It sounded like a Proton. There was a tinny rasp and a sudden jerking halt as the car came to a stop. Remembering the men from the *surau* he stepped up to the main door to greet them. In his haste he pushed in front of Mahmud who seemed equally keen to greet the first of the mourners. Instead of the men, he saw a ten-year-old Nissan Sunny taxi – an outstation taxi from Tanjong Malim – driven by a large, burly Chinese taxi-driver who looked apologetic and embarrassed. In the back seat he saw a woman with three small children. They were all boys. Each was wearing a set of cheap Batu Road T-shirts and shorts. For years thereafter, he was to remember the instant he saw the three and the shock of recognition as each of them clambered out of the shaking car. The eldest couldn't have been more than six or seven and the youngest barely three years old. Even so, their fresh young faces were marked with the undeniable parentage of their late father – that jaw, those shallow, fish-like eyes. Turning away from the woman and her brood, Tajuddeen walked away. He marched through the kitchen, brushing past Ani and out to the back yard where he slammed his fist into the retaining wall just as he heard his brother-in-law Mahmud calling his name gleefully.

"Eh, Din, Din, come back! Look at these sons, these *waris* ..."

The Mistress

I watched, from my hidden vantage point, the sharp measured steps of the concierge as he strode past the hotel's glass sliding doors. Outside, a car, sleek and shiny, paused for breath like an animal and a door was flung open – the distended jaw of a python, panting. I watched as a middle-aged woman, a Malay lady in a silk *baju kurung*, struggled to free herself from its open jaw. She levered herself out, only to fall back again. An arm was extended, almost desperately, clutching at the car door with a claw-like grip. Firm and purposeful.

It was a wonder that she didn't fall back again, though there was a moment, when, tottering on her spindly heels, her ballooning bulk seemed to lose its assurance and sway, nonchalantly at first, and then more worryingly from side to side. She had a pair of shopping bags in her hand filled to the brim with loose lengths of silk material. Listening to her instructions carefully, the concierge took them from her. And as he did, he steadied her swaying bulk with a carefully placed hand that was both correct and intimate, like the touch of a nurse. When she was squarely and firmly on the ground, she sashayed through the welcoming blasts of cooled air, into the hotel lobby.

She was fat and soft, though she still possessed a discernible waist that seemed more a desperate plea of a vain woman than a reflection of reality. There were hips and breasts too, now abundantly fleshy, sagging against the silk. She walked with assurance – the soft, dimpled flesh of her inner thighs dragging against themselves. The thought made me wince. Her face was of a form, now all too rarely seen – beautiful, proud, brazen and yet motherly. The folds of her dress traced the expanded contours of her body. The *baju* was made of Italian silk, a white background upon which fleur-de-lis and equestrian emblems were printed. Her hair was swept back in the style preferred by Malay princesses of a certain age –

swept back off the forehead; a groomed and considered coiffure, stiff with lacquer and hair-spray. Even her tussle with the python had not disturbed that.

We had arranged to meet here. She was my father's mistress. I had heard of her, and, on occasion, even seen her in the company of loud, powerful men who scattered the hungry young men like me in their wake. I don't know why I chose to ring her up (or rather, I do, but I am embarrassed for it, and, well, it is another story, more complicated). But the week before, I had picked up the telephone receiver and dialled her number. She had answered herself. I had been so surprised that I had very nearly replaced the receiver. She spoke first.

"Yes, Datin Zeraphina here." She was out of breath as she cooed her improbable name down the receiver. It was a well-known fact that she had been named 'Siti' by her parents, simple rice-farmers from Pasir Mas, renaming herself 'Zeraphina' on her arrival in Kuala Lumpur, all those years ago, as a *ronggeng* girl at the Excelsior Cabaret. According to my aunts, 'Zeraphina' had been a brand of cheap soap, rather like 'LUX', which had been heavily promoted in the early fifties. My aunts, who made a point of knowing such things, had added that the soap brand had been discontinued in the late sixties when the Chinese manufacturer had been discovered adding pig fat to the tallow used to make the soap – a fact that would have pleased my mother had she cared to find out.

"Datin, my name is Mahmud, Mahmud Mokhtar. I believe you knew my father, Mokhtar Mirzan." There was a long pause before she replied.

"Mokhtar's son, what a delight. Of course, I knew your father. We were the best of friends. Dear, sweet, Mokhtar. It's been so long, since he died."

"Yes, it has. I would like to talk with you. I have some papers of his and I …" There was another pause (only this time it was longer) and a slight intake of breath that lasted a moment too long, just long enough for me to register what I meant: that I wasn't a friend, that I ... meant trouble.

"I think that would be a very good idea, and soon."

"When are you free, Datin?"

"Dear boy, I am always free. I am a widow now, and a lady of leisure. We pray and go to Mecca, in droves."

I laughed and so did she. The true meaning of my telephone call was passed over: we both knew what I was after.

Which brings me to why I was in the lobby of a hotel so overlaid with marble that it resembled the innards of a dragon, the veins frozen, their contents a jade green tincture. I had taken the precaution of placing myself behind the large bouquet of silk flowers, each bloom a fork of the dragon's tongue – so that I could watch her as she entered.

She crossed the belly of the dragon, or rather, she marched – her purposefulness clear in the authority of her gait. There was something about her that reminded me of a warrior going into battle – "Kelantanese women", my mother would have said, "they're all like that. You marry one and I'll disown you". It was not the progress of a society lady about to meet a contemporary's son or a nephew. There was the scent of conflict in the way she negotiated her way towards the coffee shop.

I don't know now what I had expected. The flamboyant *baju* and the determined, gladiatorial approach frightened me. Shit! It made me reconsider why I was doing all this. If she had been a smaller, meeker figure dressed in a less confident manner, I might not have stopped to think. But even as I did, I knew that I could not *not* go through with the meeting. I had promised.

I followed her into the restaurant, was greeted by the same waitress who had welcomed her, and was led through to her table. She stood, I bowed. Not knowing what to do, I shook her hand as if she was a business acquaintance. She motioned with her left hand, across her ample stomach, to the chair on her right.

"Please sit on my right. The hearing in my left ear is poor. Do remove your jacket – you're not in the office now, young man." Nodding, I did, thinking to myself, "Is this how it felt to be her lover? To be solicited, cared for and attended to?" Because if it was, I could feel myself enjoying it already.

"You are so much like dear Mokhtar. I last saw him the night before his heart-attack. But don't tell your mother. How he died of a heart-attack, I don't know."

She let her eyes rest on my face. I don't know whether the tears were real but I could see them gathering in the corners of her eyes. She wasn't asking for sympathy; it was a declaration. She wanted me to know that she had loved him.

"They told me when I was playing golf. One of the caddies, or was it ... yes, it was Tengku Maizah. She loved him, too. She tried, but he never wanted her. I think they all loved him. Do they love you, too?"

She turned to me again, placing her hand on mine and smiling enquiringly.

"Yes ... maybe ... no ... I guess so ... you know."

She had divined a weakness. I felt trapped and embarrassed. After such a disclosure I could not lie and yet I had not come here to exchange confidences.

If at that moment I had weakened in my resolve and allowed myself to feel sympathy for her, I would have left the table feeling lighter in myself but burdened down by the knowledge that I had betrayed my mother. Datin Zeraphina sensed the conflict within me and chose not to force her lover's son to have to make the choice. Her experience prevailed; she elected to wait out the test.

"Well, I'm having mee soup. I am forbidden fried foods, sweet foods, oily foods – in fact, any food save boiled foods. And I am sure you know how dull that can be. Oh, dear boy! You are so much like Mokhtar."

She looked at me and smiled.

It was an open, guileless smile. There were dimples on her cheeks and creases where her make-up had smeared.

I felt then as he must have felt before me, softened and lost to her charm. This woman, this courtesan, nothing more in fact than a common whore; a woman who could open beer bottles with her pudenda, host orgies into the night that exhausted the city of all her sins, and still awaken the next morning to take breakfast on the verandah of the Polo Club after a gallop on one of her racehorses. This woman had won me. She had slept with kings and princes, ministers and saints, and enchanted them all. What was I by comparison?

"You must tell me about yourself. You must tell me about your brothers and sisters. 1 knew all about you, you know. Your father and I would talk for hours about each of you in turn. You mustn't think he didn't love you just because he didn't stay at home. He told me about the time a fish-bone got stuck in your throat and you cried so much that he rushed you off to the hospital, only to find that the bone had been dislodged by the time you had reached the hospital.

"Does that surprise you? He knew that Mas was unhappy at boarding school, but never expected that she would turn to drugs. He wasn't ashamed by the publicity so much as by his own neglect. You have all got a great deal to learn about him. He lost touch. Your mother and he became strangers to one another. Your home, that house in Section 16, became her house. He felt that he wasn't wanted, wasn't needed. He never felt that with me."

"No, I imagine not."

I was sharper than I intended to be, remembering my allegiances with a stab of pain. She was pushed onto the defensive.

"It wasn't as you think. We loved each other. He wanted to marry me, but he wouldn't unless your mother agreed to a divorce. She refused. I am sure you know that. I think she was afraid that he would have forgotten about all of you, neglected you. I wouldn't have allowed him to. You see, I couldn't have any more children by then."

"I'm sorry."

"It was a long time ago. Talking to you now brings it all back to life. He was an exciting man, your father. I think he would have been pleased that you called me. In fact, he left some things with me and I know that he would have wanted them to have gone to you or your brother."

With that she slipped her hand into her crocodile skin handbag and fished out a pair of gold cufflinks studded with diamonds in the form of 'MM'. I knew she was lying. But I didn't care. Nor did I care that I had seen the same cufflinks, unmarked by diamonds, in K.M. Oli Mohamed only the day before. Her presumption was total. Her gall and verve inestimable.

"May I give them to you?"

"I couldn't." But I knew I could. "But you must accept them, they're your father's. He would have wanted one of you to have them."

"Oh, very well." My resolve crumpled as I rolled the cufflinks between my fingers and watched the diamonds glint in the light.

"And in turn I must ask you for those silly letters. I trust you didn't show them to your mother?"

I shook my head. But I, too, was lying. My mother had shown them to me, her eyes red with the pain, her face raw with anger. The scene that followed had resulted in my interview with the city's most famous courtesan. She had made me vow that I would exact some kind of revenge. Had I not promised, she would have kept on at me indefinitely. I said a great deal, too much in fact. She would not have stopped crying otherwise.

Datin Zeraphina, or 'Siti', the rice-farmer's daughter from Pasir Mas, reached across to the letters, her plump little hands encrusted with rubies and diamonds. She tugged at them. There was a moment's indecision and I retained my grip before letting go. And then they were hers.

She had outmanoeuvred me. I knew there would be trouble later. My mother would accuse me of being like my father, faithless and worthless. Poor mother, to have married a man only to have him meet a woman such as Datin Zeraphina. Mother's world was bounded by deception and betrayal, all of it stemming from this one woman. The letters were in her hands, tied up with one of those pink ribbons father used in his legal offices. They still harboured the scent of jasmine and sandalwood, stored in sequence, preserved by a man we had all thought, all those years ago, beyond love.

She gathered them in her arms, with the delicacy only a beloved can understand, at once solicitous, peremptory and all-consuming. Looking at me in silent triumph, she kissed them.

"I loved him and he loved me. If you had read the letters you will know. You think me no better than a common whore. No, don't pretend, don't shake your head. I know. I understand. I have never tried to deny my past. I was a *ronggeng* girl – it's true. I'm not embarrassed. Your father was the one man who loved me beyond anything else. His love redeemed me. He saved me and these letters are the testament.

"Your mother, though, must never know about them. It is better for her to think I was a whore and nothing more. I cannot deprive her now of her memories of Mokhtar. I hope you understand. Good. I am glad.

"But we mustn't talk anymore about Mokhtar or I will cry. I am old now and dwell in the past too much. Tell me about yourself. Is it true that you are seeing the Zulkarnain girl?"

And it was in this vein that the lunch continued. At two o'clock she called for the bill, paid despite my protests and let me escort her to the front of the hotel to await her chauffeur. That was the last I saw of her. She died a month later. I did not attend the funeral.

My mother didn't speak to me for a year after the lunch. She accused me of betraying her and accepted no explanation. Months later, at a family wedding, one of my aunts took me aside. At the time she told me that she wanted to speak to me about something quite important. Her face was wreathed in smiles. Once away from the crowds, she confronted me with my actions. Did I know that Datin Zeraphina had staggered from her deathbed to see me and that she had told half the city that Mokhtar's son was blackmailing her? Did I know that? Did I not know when to leave things alone?

I was wearing the cufflinks that night. I am now too attached to them. I don't care that the money spent on them was intended for her son's education. I will not return them. They are a mark of a woman's vanity, her fears and pride. A fierce mixture of forces had dragged her from her deathbed to talk about her love and gather back to her her lost youth and her lost loves in a flourish of generosity and cunning that had left me breathless. Maybe I am more like my father than I thought. My mother was right – we've all betrayed her.

Sara and the Wedding

"Kak Tipah, I really don't mind Shahnaz marrying before me. Azman's such a good man – how can I mind?" There was a note of resignation in Sara's voice as if she were tired of answering the same question again and again. Kak Tipah, her elder and similarly unmarried cousin, shook her head in disbelief. She had an instinctual grasp of her cousin Sara's weaknesses and she replied in an insinuating manner, prodding Sara with her forefinger as she spoke.

"Are you sure? I would hate it. Absolutely hate it. I'd insist on a Louis Vuitton cabin-bag in recompense. Not a fake one – mind you. A real one, with LV, LV, LV everywhere," she said, lingering on the letters of the logo.

"You know I'm not like that, Kak Tipah. I want my sister to be happy. So what if she marries before me? It's not as if I can't find a man." Since Sara was both plump and homely, her argument sounded as hollow as a *tempayan* jar at midday and she knew it. Sara had long since grown accustomed to glaring differences between the fabled *Sara Fakaruddin: Advocate and Solicitor* of her name card and the sweaty, short-of-breath, hair-thinning, late thirty-something woman she in fact was.

This was not to say she conceded defeat immediately. She was a fighter, at the start. And, in a campaign as nerve-wrecking as any jungle warfare – the British could have learnt a thing or two from her – she tried her best to make the jungle 'her' friend. But her implements of war differed from those of the sweaty soldiers – non-drip mascara, ruby red lipstick, *urut* sessions at dawn and corsets so tight that once she'd fainted in the middle of the Bankruptcy Court.

In her early days at the Bar she had worn short black pencil-skirts and high-heels that had made her look more like a disco-*dangdut* GRO than a rising advocate. However, after a succession of desperate rearguard skirmishes at twenty-two, twenty-five and twenty-eight inches matching the ill-fated British in Kuala Kangsar, Tanjung Malim and Batu Pahat respectively, she knew the worst – she was doomed. Cellulite was her future. Surging ahead ferociously like bicycle-riding Japanese warriors the cellulite clung to her thighs, her waist, her belly and her buttocks. And, much like the British before her, who realised only too late that Singapore's anti-artillery barrage faced in the wrong direction, she too was forced to sue for peace, accepting an ignominious defeat and the world of elasticated *baju kurungs*. Relinquishing the pleasures of the youth, Sara at the age of twenty-nine entered the inner sanctum of the *mak cik*-dom.

Her elder cousin, sensing an opportunity, seized it with all the vigour of a market-holder wringing a chicken's neck.

"I can see it in your eyes when you look at Azman. He's tall, he's good-looking, he's an MCKK boy and he's a lawyer from Kelantan – your father's state. I can see it all. *Aku tahu*: you don't have to tell me." She spelled out Azman's attractions on her fingers as if she were weighing up the attractions of a length of *kain songket* or a Sime UEP house.

"So what? He's not the only Kelantanese lawyer in the country. Plus, I don't know how you can 'see' anything. I love Azman like a brother. I consider the subject closed." Lina was pleased by the spiritedness of her reply and she looked at her cousin confidently. Kak Tipah had an awfully irritating manner.

"Well, I'm not the only one who thinks you look a unhappy. My mother thinks the same as well." Kak Tipah wrinkled her nose unpleasantly as she spoke. Lina flushed at the mention of her aunt and stiffened perceptibly.

"I have things to do, Kak Tipah. These *bunga telur* have to be placed on the VIP tables," she said pointedly. However, her anger had got the better of her and she added, "You and Mak Cik Zainah can think whatever you want to think. I really don't give a damn! *Aku tak kisah!*" With that she scooped the *bunga telur* from the table and stormed off.

Cradling the *bunga telur* in her arms, Sara marched out of the study and onto the verandah which was now enclosed, if not strangled by an extensive ring of corrugated iron roofing – sheltering rows of tables and chairs ready for the night's guests. The unremitting glare of fluorescent lights left the metal tables looking hard and ugly, the chairs flimsy and awkward and she turned away, dispiritedly. Frustrated by the sight and reminded of her 'single', unmarried state, she glanced inside the house again where she caught sight of the bridal *pelamin*, arrayed in gold. She sighed as she studied it, a deep sigh that betrayed, at least for a moment, a trace of what her cousin had been accusing her of. She gazed at the two chairs and swallowed pensively. 'If only', she thought, 'if only things could be different'. Sara couldn't quite dispel a surge of sadness, a wistfulness so keen it almost made her shiver.

Realising, despite her lowness, the dangers of such a train of thought she shook her head severely. She hated succumbing to her family's insinuations and she was determined not to ruin the evening by thinking of what Kak Tipah had said to her.

"Dammit," she whispered to herself, "here I am, a bloody lawyer who can reduce prosecution witnesses and policemen to tears, fretting over my *tak guna punya* family. I must pull myself together. They are not going to get the better of me." She was still a fighter.

In an effort to distract herself, she stepped back into the house and strode towards the *pelamin*. Work, as she had discovered in the past, was its own reward, its own merciful distraction. She was going to check the wretched *pelamin* one last time. Fixing her attention on the dais, she dared it (and by extension her cousin) to taunt her any longer. She was in charge now and her concerned but superior expression fended off all such doubts. If she heard just one more remark, she'd give whoever it was a piece of her mind. That she would.

Reassured by her anger, she looked at the cushions that had been placed on both the chairs – she'd bought them herself from

Kamdars on Jalan Tuanku Abdul Rahman. Having checked to see that they were attractively placed and fluffed up nicely, she turned her attention to the embroidered-applique fans which the *pengapits* were to carry. She bit her lip as she thought of the *pengapits*. She was to have been one but her mother, in a moment of supreme thoughtlessness, had told her she was too fat – 'Cannot have you so fat, fat up there. What will people say? *Nanti,* later *susah* to *kahwinkan* you, Sara'.

She turned away from the fans and looked at the gold material that had been pinned to the *pelamin*. The material cascaded from the back of the dais in a spray of loose, elegant folds, the gold shimmering under a carefully located spotlight. She had to concede that the effect was really very attractive. Kak Tipah who, despite her poisonous tongue, had been in charge of pinning the material onto the canopy had acquitted herself well. However, suddenly she realised that the folds were uneven. Squinting, she checked the *pelamin* again, tilting her head as she did.

Alamak! She stepped back in shock. The *pelamin* was uneven. The folds on the right were longer, more voluptuous and generous than those on the left. What could she do? What should she do? Should she call her mother? Shahnaz? Kak Tipah? Checking her watch she saw that it was already half past six. Realising the time – or rather the lack of time – she panicked. It would all be her fault. She'd get into trouble. She was supposed to have supervised Kak Tipah and now she'd failed. Her mother and all her aunts would *marah* her – they'd shout at her and complain. They'd tell her it was just typical of her – all these career women who were too busy to bother with *pelamins*, weddings and the really important things in life, the things that young women were supposed to spend their time thinking about.

She had half an hour to unpin the material, straighten it and then repin it. Half an hour. It wasn't possible: half an hour to unpin six feet of material. Deflated by the task in hand, she fell to her knees, allowing the *bunga telur* in her arms to roll across the floor. She felt tears in her eyes at the unfairness of it all. Here she was dashing about, worrying about her sister's wedding when, in actual fact, the mere thought of it made her feel unwanted and ashamed. Why should she care that Shahnaz's *pelamin* was uneven? It wasn't her *bersanding*. She was the fat, unwanted elder sister, the one they laughed at behind their hands. She was the one who was expected to grow old and useless on a steady diet of loneliness and solitude. They didn't seem to care that she supported half the family, that she had her own successful legal practice, that outside the home she was respected and admired. Damn them, they didn't care – she was just the fat-fat one who was still unmarried.

Just then she heard Kak Tipah's voice in the kitchen. She was shouting at the caterers and her voice was raised in an ugly screech.

"*Apalah ini* – so salty and the *ayam* only *buntut*! We pay you so much and all we get is *buntut*?" Her cousin's presence nearby immediately instilled in her a sense of urgency. She wasn't going to let the woman see her like this. She wasn't going to let her think she'd won. No way! Willing herself back in control of her emotions, she wiped her face and patted her temples as if forcing the tears back into the tear ducts. She picked up the *bunga telur* one by one and then stood up. Resolutely and without a smidgen of doubt she told herself, 'It's too late to do anything, just too late and it's not my fault: it's not my problem'. The guests were expected in the next hour and they couldn't possibly unpin the material now. Her determination to ignore the lopsided material made her smile for a moment, her face creasing up with a mixture of embarrassment and a resolute stubbornness.

Who cared what Azman's family would think? Who cared? Certainly not her, not Sara, the one they all took for granted. Her mother? Hah! As if she bothered. And her sister, Shahnaz? Well, Shahnaz the lovely, willowy bride would have to endure sitting on a *pelamin* that was unevenly decorated. Hah! So the girl did have her flaws. It was enough to make her laugh out loud – poor Shahnaz. There had to be some drawbacks to marrying Azman.

Turning away from the *pelamin* she walked out of the sitting room and back onto the verandah. Her head felt lighter – it was as if her selfishness, her decision not to do anything about the *pelamin*, not to bother about the tiresome wedding and what the relatives thought, had freed her of some hitherto unnamed burden. She'd thrown off something painful and inexpressible – ripped it from within herself and discarded it. Freed of her doubts and the sour tang of bitterness that Kak Tipah had exposed within her, she suddenly felt ready, willing and open. But open for what? She paused. Suddenly she was afraid. Was she sure that there was anything out there? Would there be anything waiting for her – the ungainly, unfashionable sister? Or rather would there be anybody waiting for her – a nice young man like Azman, maybe?

She knew that the sliver of hope was too valuable to be discarded and she willed, almost desperately, herself to believe in it, utterly and implicitly. She assured herself that there was something out there waiting for her – something, maybe even somebody fine, noble and exciting. Yes, she thought, vowing to herself with a passionate averment, there'll be an Azman for me, too; only he'll be brighter, more charming and less arrogant. Emboldened by this hope, she breathed in deeply, savouring her confident discovery and the pleasure it gave her.

Standing now on the edge of the verandah she gazed out beyond the serried ranks of the tables and chairs at the garden, past the waiters dashing frantically from one table to another checking the place settings. And though the air was heavy and humid, she imagined a wisp-like breeze licking her face. She closed her eyes and willed, if not beckoned in her mind, the growing animation of the house, its inhabitants and helpers, to come to her. She opened up her senses up to the raw, bubbling cacophony – the preparations, the shouts from the kitchen, the laughter of her male cousins, a pungent melange of chuckles, sniggers, cackles and shrieks that rushed around her before enveloping her in a crashing wave of sound that swamped her, leaving her immobile and inert and yet happy and excited. As the sounds ebbed, Sara was left with an impression of richness as well as a desperate desire to partake in that abundance. Everything seemed alloyed with gold, impenetrable but rich with opportunities. She turned to face the garden and breathed in the air again. Swallowing the thick, heavy air she said to herself, 'Damn them. I'm going to enjoy myself'.

She dropped the *bunga telur* nonchalantly onto one of the VIP tables and sauntered off into the garden, oblivious to the small imperfections in the table settings, the dirty napkins and the squishy mud underfoot. Without shoes or slippers, she stepped deliberately into the murky pools of rainwater, splashing her *baju* and her calves. She shrugged and walked on until she was standing beyond the covered area, under the jackfruit trees at the bottom of the garden. She seemed unaware of the mosquitoes that buzzed around her, brushing them off her face and arms. Looking up into the foliage, her eyes settled on the ripening jackfruit wrapped in pink plastic bags. They were large and bulbous and she gazed at them, marvelling at their size and the sweet pungency of their scent. It was a rich, heady perfume that seeped into her lungs, accelerating the pumping of her heart as it worked its way through her entire body.

Suddenly, everything around her seemed more alive and she blinked at the small fairy lights that glowed in the heavily leafed trees. There was an unreal aura to the silent patches of garden that were thus swathed in light. Standing in the dark she watched the pool of light swaying with the wind. They danced magically as she hummed a soft half-remembered song. Enjoying the lights with as much pleasure as a three-year-old, she failed to notice the soft, confident tread of her second cousin, Ramli.

"What are you doing out here, Sara?" He asked in Malay.

"Heh! Ramli, don't surprise me like that. I was thinking."

"Sorry," he said, lowering his eyes as he apologised. She knew she'd hurt his feelings and she apologised in turn.

"I didn't mean to scold you. Don't worry. I was just surprised by you. I was thinking, that was all – just thinking." However she felt embarrassed by her outburst and she patted his cheek softly with the back of her hand.

He raised his eyes to hers and smiled. It was a simple open smile.

"Thinking?" he asked, his voice laced with a note of self-deprecation. "You're all so clever, you KL girls. Not like me. I'm just a *kampung* boy. Yes, you're always thinking. I admire you so much."

"Me? Really." It was Sara's turn to be surprised.

"Why not? You're clever, hard-working and *baik*. I read about you in the newspapers defending Datuks and Tan Sri's. You are famous. Everyone respects Kak Sara."

"Oh? I'm touched," she said half-bemused. She tried looking away but Ramli, sensing her mood, caught her eye, holding her eye for a few seconds longer than their cousinage necessitated. Finally he spoke.

"See how you looked after your family when your father died. You're *baik* – so good," he added, his voice full of awed admiration. Sara shook her head.

"No, it was nothing. Any daughter would have done it. I just fulfilled my duty."

"You are modest, too."

"Ramli, Ramli, Ramli," she said, half-hoping that her friendly, if impersonal tone of voice would ease the growing intimacy, unfurling the darkness around them. Once again she tried looking away but he stood in front of her, blocking her view of the house – shielding the light and screening the familiar voices.

"Were you thinking of me, I wonder?" he asked, pressing her hand warmly as he spoke. His plump hand, though sweaty, was reassuring.

"You're so self-centred, Ramli," she replied jokingly. Blushing pleasantly, she smiled despite herself. It was flattering to be followed into the garden even if it was only Ramli. She looked at him more closely and saw that he wasn't unattractive. He was a little heavy around the waist and his skin was pock-marked and florid. Despite this he had dark, deep-set eyes and a moustache that was thick and generous.

"I think it was me, wasn't it?" he repeated, widening his eyes and pouting as he spoke.

"Maybe," she added enigmatically, trying to stifle her laughter. She felt as if she'd stepped into a TV soap opera, a creaky *Cerekarama*.

"I've been watching you." Ramli smirked as he spoke. Just then he leant forward.

"Give me a kiss? Just one? There's no need to be shy. Nobody can see. I know you want it. What's one kiss?" he implored as he brushed his lips along the nape of her neck. Unthinkingly she stretched her neck to receive his attention, yielding for a moment at least to his advances. As she succumbed, she felt his hand pressing against the rise of her breasts and then squeezing her forcefully. His lips were warm and sticky and he smelt of stale *kretek* and *budu*. She gasped silently as he massaged her erect breasts.

"Hot-*lah*, you. I want you," he whispered hoarsely. However his words shook her from her reverie. Hearing him moan and feeling his penis pressed up against her belly she suddenly felt afraid. With a struggle she managed to extricate herself.

"You're like a teenager," she said, stiffly pushing him away with a fierce shove.

"You want it," he muttered angrily. Ignoring him, she brushed the creases out of her *baju* in silence and quickly retraced her steps. Ramli, waiting beneath the trees in the half-shadows, watched her enter the kitchen area before he emerged from the dark and slipped into the house via the sitting room.

Back in the house and far from the unsettling glow of the garden lights, Sara picked her way through the vats of prepared food, stepping over trays of curry, vermillion-coloured rose water and oily fried chicken. Sitting in the midst of the food and the preparations was Sara's favourite aunt, Mak Cik Khatijah, who was unafraid to admit to working for a living. She squatted under a makeshift shelter, her hair covered by a simple scarf, stirring a vat of bubbling buffalo *rendang*.

"Sara!" she called, "stop your fretting and sit with me. Take this paddle and stir the *rendang*. Mak Cik is tired." Her aunt, despite her appearance, spoke excellent English – a testament to her convent education, English that was peppered with Malay.

"*Kahwin, kahwin-lah*! What's the big deal. You young women think men are so special. But I tell all my nieces and that includes you, that men are good for only two things. The first is sex and the second is entertainment. *Main-main saja*: just good for a bit of fun – but don't take home." Mak Cik Khatijah's bluntness was an enormous relief after her surprise encounter with Ramli.

"No-*lah*, Mak Cik."

"Two or three minutes, then they're over. They think it's so special – all that grunting and moaning. *Aiyah*, after they're forty they can only manage it once a month and then for only one minute. Pap! And it's over."

Stirring the *rendang*, which was thick and heavy, Sara asked, "Then why do they remarry, Mak Cik?"

"If they have money, like your uncle before, they want to show off the size of their balls. If the second wife is young and hot, then they are hot, too."

"Mak Cik! You are shocking."

"I'm not shocking, Sara – the world is. Men are like *budak kecil*, only. Little boys want toys, only."

"Even uncle?"

"Especially your uncle. Your uncle could just about do it once a month. Hah! Who do you think fathered his new son? The driver-*lah*. I say take a man and treat him like he'd treat you. *Buat dulu*, only with the handsome one and then you get rid of them: Kelantanese style." Mak Cik Khatijah sniggered to herself.

"At *bersandings* they all look so cute, like Azman. *Sayang* only their wives. *Cium-cium* and *hormat-hormat*. Yes, *sayang*; no, *sayang*. Then they change. You're not missing anything, Sara. Eh, stir it properly, otherwise it will stick to the bottom."

"Actually, I'd better change, Mak Cik."

"Put on your nice *baju*, Sara? Not the frumpy ones. They're for ladies like me. You must enjoy yourself, you know. Experiment. Don't listen to your cousins and your other aunts – they're all so full of themselves. Smug. *Cakap-cakap tak serupa bikin*. They think they are so special. You know, don't you, what I mean?"

"Yes, Mak Cik." With that Sara bounced up from where she'd been squatting and dashed into the house. By now the house was beginning to pulse with activity as the caterers fought their way past the florists and the video-cameramen. At the foot of the main staircase, she bumped into Ramli again who made a point of rubbing his hands against her thighs as she stepped away from him.

"Eeeh," she said under breath threateningly, "you keep your hands to yourself, Ramli."

"Difficult, your body is calling me. I can smell you everywhere. You want me to touch you," he whispered in return. Scowling, she darted up the staircase without looking back at him.

The rest of the evening went surprisingly well. Many of the women sighed as they observed the bridal couple. Shahnaz was poised and beautiful, her slender waist accentuated by her sequin-encrusted *baju*. Alongside her, Azman's six-foot frame seemed magnificent and confident. Sitting silently in state during the *bersanding* ceremony, they were a pair of divine spirits: mute sentinels of the evening's pleasures. The food, too, was highly praised. Many of the guests, surprised and privately rather relieved to be entertained at home, found themselves enjoying the *bersanding* all the more because of its informality and warmth. As a result many of them stayed on until well after midnight – long after the departure of the VIPs. They laughed and chatted whilst lying on *mengkuang* mats that had been unrolled in the living room. Sara, her sisters and the servants plied them with coffee, Malay cakes, Sumatran cheroots and betel nut so strong it made one of the cousins fall into a deep sleep.

Sara, for her part, had been in charge of collecting and storing the presents and by the end of the evening, two monstrous piles of gifts, both as tall as herself, were on display in the entrance hall. She had greeted countless people during the evening, salaaming them with great warmth and exuberance. Some had even whispered to the aunts that maybe, Sara was in love herself. Kak Tipah told herself that her cousin must have discovered a new recipe for cheesecake or a one-size fits all, super kaftan.

By 1.30 in the morning, however, most of the guests had returned home, leaving the family to open the presents amongst themselves. Shahnaz and Azman – in great contrast to their earlier passivity – had thrown themselves into the task, ripping open the gaily coloured paper and tossing it aside. As her sister and new brother-in-law waded their way through their toasters, Corningware, Queen Anne silverware and rice cookers like a pair of flying squirrels, Sara withdrew to the study and from there she slipped out of the house and into the garden where she waited under the same tembusu tree that she had stood under earlier that evening.

Unbeknownst to her family she had been watching Ramli discreetly all evening, observing the way he scratched his belly after the *makan*, rubbed his ear-lobes repeatedly as he talked and rearranged his balls each time he shifted on his seat. That made her smile as she remembered their little encounter under the tree and his firm insistence. It allowed her to forgive him his wife and three children, his mediocre job in a small finance company in Kota Bharu and his ramshackle Proton Saga – all things that would have shocked

Kak Tipah to her core. Whilst Ramli, in truth, hovered on the periphery of the *bersanding* as far as everyone else was concerned, his stealthy, if slightly ungainly presence, had been central to her interests. And, in the growing excitement of the night, she realised that he, too, was watching her. She carried out her duties with added zest because she knew he was watching her. She could feel the heat of his eyes on her – watching her, following her and waiting. Knowing that he was tracing her movements between the kitchen, the study, the VIP tables and the *pelamin* filled her with a delicious sense of being desired. She knew what it was like to be wanted.

Within minutes she found herself in a familiar, if secluded, corner of the garden. She had found herself under the same trees as if borne along by a wave of mounting desire. Unstoppable and sweeping, it had impelled her to return to her earlier position. Standing alone, resting her head against the trunk of the tree, she stared up into the dark sky at the stars. Yes, she thought, the heavens are fair and life – life was so varied, beautiful and passionate. Just then he reappeared.

"You are back," he said half-whispering.

"Yes. I am." With that she felt an unburdening like nothing she'd ever felt before. She allowed her body to go limp, succumbing entirely to Ramli, his presence, his uneven teeth, his acrid body odour and his maleness. She felt the rough firmness of Ramli's hands on her body as he loosened her *baju* and pressed himself expertly against her. As he proceeded to undo her bra and massage her bulging breasts, she wondered if indeed it was her body being so exquisitely mauled. Was this living, she wondered dreamily?

"Hot," he muttered, repeating the word again and again into her ear as she arched her back. She wanted to say 'no' but her voice was too weak. Mouthing the word to herself she tried to protest. But years of denial and lack of interest prevented her. Her needs were too great. Something deep within her asserted itself – crying out 'yes'. Within minutes it was all over. Still shaking from the pleasurable onslaught, she shivered deliciously. Her *baju* was down by her knees and her bra tangled up. Dishevelled, she leant back against the tree as Ramli hurriedly zipped up his flies. "When shall we meet again?" Ramli asked urgently.

"Never," she replied. There was a distracted half-smile on her face. She had achieved all she wanted and now it was her turn to assert herself. Casting her eyes upwards, she screwed them up and started screaming. This, she knew, would prove everything to her family. This would prove her true desirability, her power.

"Rape, rape!"

Go East!

The people here used to ask me what I did to deserve this posting: "Why-uh, Lahad Datu, you *gila* or something?" It was a rhetorical question – one of those things that people, especially planters, say after they've had too much to drink. They say it seriously enough but that doesn't mean they want an answer – and that's one of the first things I learnt about these people: they don't want answers. In the early days when I first arrived, I used to reply. But I was green then. Chan, the bartender at the Planter's Club, used to say, "*Mahmud, kau* stoo-pid like *kerbau.*"

In the early days I'd pause for a while, like a good student, and then explain why I had chosen to come to Lahad Datu. I'd mention the soil types (the soil's this rich volcanic mix that's high in nutrients), the cocoa yields (because of the soil you don't need so much fertiliser) and the climate. Cocoa's also an interesting crop to work with: it's so delicate and risk-prone that you spend most of the time trying to figure out ways to avoid your next catastrophe. Once you've tried cocoa, my lecturer used to say, you'll never want to go back to oil palm: it's intellectually satisfying. It makes me wince now to think of it, to think how I must have sounded. But they'd laugh and brush me aside with a snort, "Huh, *Budak-lah!*" Behind the bar with his beer glasses Chan would shake his head. It took me quite a while to realise I wasn't at Agricultural College any more.

It was only later then that I understood them better. They had come all the way to Lahad Datu because they wanted to escape from questions; they wanted to be free. Replies which may have led to answers – new ideas, solutions or conclusions – were the last thing they wanted to hear. I used to think that people asked questions because they were in search of something, so that they'll get answers – answers that would teach them something, you know, enlighten them. Like me. In those days I was always haunted by questions, questions, questions about myself, my mother and my future.

These fellows didn't want to be enlightened: they wanted confirmation and that was all; they wanted to be confirmed in what they knew. Questions were statements of fact they chose to word in a different manner. They had given up on questions and doubts years before: that's why they were here, in Lahad Datu. And when you drink as much as they do, words become an irrelevance – like the foam on the top of your Anchor beer: nice to look at but tasteless; and conversation is what punctuates the pauses in between the beers.

They'd laugh and shout in my face. "Hah," they'd say, "Mahmud wanted to come here. He's not bad like the rest of us; just stupid." Then they'd slam down their empty glasses on the counter and order more. They'd say that but I knew they were impressed. They wouldn't have admitted it, but they were, they were dead impressed.

You see, most of them were here because they were useless; rejects, the kind of fellows that would always be getting into trouble in the Peninsula – oversleeping, overdrinking, screwing the boss's wife or slipping their hands into the cash-till. You know the kind of thing – younger brothers, unwanted cousins and forgotten family members (the ones everyone *wants* to forget). They had been sent off to Agricultural College 'to be sorted out'. Which, of course, didn't happen. It never does. None of them ever wanted to be planters. Not like me.

They're always complaining – about the work, the pay, the company and the locals. They spend all their time dreaming about KL or Penang. But I know they're really running away from it all. They say they love KL and the Peninsula but within a week of home leave they're dying to get back to Sandakan or Lahad Datu.

I'm different though. I chose to become a planter, an agronomist. You see, I've got my career all mapped out. I've always wanted to be just what I am now – a plantation manager and I've worked for it. I'm organised and hard-working: that's me. That's why the company employed me – I'm their youngest plantation manager. I'm not proud or anything but I'm happy doing what I'm doing and I'm good at it.

I'm from Petaling Jaya originally. Yes, I'm a city boy and I know we're not supposed to want to be farmers or anything as boring as plantation managers, but I've never wanted to be anything else. When I was in primary school I told my friends, "I'll be a planter when I grow up". They all wanted to be lawyers or accountants. But I took one look at the accountants and their pasty, tired faces and I thought, my God, I don't want to be like them.

My father was a planter, too – one of the first Malay planters. He even studied Agricultural Science at Cirencester in Britain – though I don't know what good it did him learning about Friesian cows, arable farming and sheep gelding. He died before I was born and I never knew him. Mak has never liked to talk about him. But I've got a photograph; he's in his solar topee, his starched shorts and his cotton shirt. You could say it's always been a dream of mine to look like that myself.

I like Sabah. I liked it from the day I arrived. I think I liked it even before I arrived. I knew it was going to be different and it was. It was noisy, dirty, rough and un-Malay. There are fewer bloody Protons (God, I hate that car) and loads of jeeps, four-wheel drives and small trucks piled high with bags of fertiliser, belching out diesel fumes.

If you're like me and sick of the stuffiness of KL, Sabah is a kind of relief, a place where you can spit in the streets and no one cares: you're not expected to be one thing or another. You don't have to attend endless bloody boring *kenduris* of relatives you hardly know. No family: it's a liberation, let's break open the *tapai*! I could have taken a job in Johor but that would have been too close to home. Maybe I'm more like the rest of the planters than I'd like to think.

I especially like Lahad Datu, the town. There's nothing fussy and precious about the town. My mother's velvet armchairs would look out of place here. It's hard, dirty and dangerous, too. You can get mugged for ten ringgit and killed for twice as much. It's full of Filipinos – they're called the 'illegals' and they're the ones who cause all the trouble. They're also the ones who make it exciting, unpredictable and edgy. There's something nice about not having too many *Melayu* about; they're always so disapproving – all that *tak boleh, tak halus, tak manis* – it makes me sick. We're not in an Istana any more and we carry on as if we're all courtiers or something.

Well, anyhow, the Filipinos – they're different. There are large groups of them at the roadside. They sit there; some of them squat, chewing betel nut and smoking *kretek*. They don't talk much to one another and they watch you closely as you walk by. Their skin is leathery and hard, like treated cowhide. They smell rancid. I think they can sense people who are careless with their money or easy to rob. They step out of the way when I walk by but I know they'd slit my throat for twenty ringgit, no problem.

Jimmy Gan, one of the old-time planters, tells me that they're Filipinos: Suluks and Bajaus. He can tell the difference between them; he talks their lingo. It sounds like Malay but the words are harder and uglier. They really respect him now, though they didn't use to initially. No one messes with his children when they're walking through town. One guy did; he was just off the *kumpit*, the dugout canoe, from Tawi-Tawi and he was never seen again. Jimmy's got a full arsenal in his house; guns like you've never seen before with latches, barrels and carbines. He's got a few repeat action machine guns. He calls them his 'girls' and he treats them better than any of the women he's had.

"The whores around here will give you the clap. Last time, my balls nearly fell off," he says. "I stick to my 'girls'. When I get horny, I go out and kill something." Jimmy's wife lives in KK because his estate is too isolated and prone to pirate raids. It may sound exciting but it's not, because they are evil bastards. The first time they came he wasn't prepared. They ransacked his house and forced him to watch while they raped his wife and each of his three daughters. Then they killed his Hainanese cook. The second time Jimmy was ready and he killed six of them. The seventh he caught (he had been shot in the leg). He tortured the man like a rat before bashing his brains out with a mallet. He hates the Filipinos and the ones who know stay well clear of him now. But I like him.

He took me to the Club on my first night and even though I was so uptight he's always been good to me. He lent me his housekeeper for the first month or so. She was a sweet-faced Timorese girl with a scar on her chin and every night after she cooked my dinner, she'd wash up and then come to my bedroom and sleep on the floor beside the bed like a dog. I guess Jimmy must have turned to something other than his 'girls' some nights. I sent her back when I caught her garrotting the pariah dog that skulked around the yard. She had broken its front legs and wired its snout. Her mouth was covered in blood and the vein on the animal's neck was still pumping out blood. I'll never forget the sound of the dog whelping.

Well, after Maria – that was her name – I got another maid. I insisted on a Muslim and got Suriya. She said she was Javanese, from Surabaya. She had that strange forehead all Javanese have, high and tilting and hands that seemed to want to dance all the time. She was very graceful in the way that poor women usually are: neat and delicate with long well-oiled hair but rough, dirt encrusted hands. She always wore a *baju kebaya* which was very tight and fitting across her buttocks and her breasts. Her breasts were like mangosteen – ready to pop at any moment. There were times when I nearly reached over and felt them.

But I was engaged already and it never seemed quite right to do anything like that in the early days. I was very prim then. The boys from the Club would always ask me to join them at the whorehouse but I never did.

"Hell, I'm engaged," I'd say and they'd laugh.

"Well, we're married and Abdul's married four times over," which was true. They were always horny and the Filipino women were only twenty bucks a 'three way'.

I guess it's the loneliness out on the estate, thinking and thinking as you're doing your rounds of inspection. I mean I think about things; abstract things, like what are we doing here and why does Allah single us out? I enjoy it, the loneliness. It's peacefulness for me. But after a while even I end up thinking about sex, though I try not to. I try to be different.

It's partly because of that, that I started going into town for the Friday prayers. I thought I'd meet some nicer, more solid family men, the kind who would understand what I was going through. I did. There was this nice Orang Sungei man, Khalid Apong, who was the manager of the Sabah Perkasa Bank. He'd take me back to his house for lunch and we'd talk – mainly politics, because everyone talks about politics here in Sabah and the differences between the Peninsula and Sabah. He would pat me on the back. "Never mind," he'd say, "we're all *Melayu*." He liked KL and Petaling Jaya especially. He pronounced the names like an Indonesian with that flat nasal intonation. He was fond of saying, "I am *halus*," refined, or rather he was always talking about refinement: there's a difference.

We got on well and he understood my problems with the guys at the Planter's Club. I told him about Farida, my fiancee and how much I loved her and how I was saving up to marry her. He was very supportive and his wife would do nice things like give me bottles of *acar* and *sambal belacan* for my dinner. I moved my account to his bank and I joined him once a week for the Koran reading session they held in his *kampung*. He introduced me to his teenage daughters whom his wife would ensure were sitting next to me at dinner. They were good people but I was beginning to feel suffocated, like in KL. And after a while I stopped visiting their house.

Anyhow it was about this time after my first home leave (I was already into my second year at the posting) that I got drunk one night. Up until then I hadn't been drinking at all. I returned home so incoherent that Suriya had to put me to bed. I think I must have pulled her in after me. Whatever it was, she was in bed with me, all over me. Her tongue and hands pressing and caressing me, her beautiful long hair draped across the sheets. Either I was drunk or I was scared but I didn't do anything. I lay there like a fool and cried afterwards.

Suriya seemed to understood without me having to explain anything. She wasn't upset. She held me and patted me as I cried. I think she thought I was sad or miserable. But I wasn't. I was angry, angry with myself for my uselessness and my inability to give it to her good and proper, to have her moaning on the floor like Abdul and Jimmy would've done to her. After an hour she left me and returned to her room.

I was so tired that I fell asleep almost immediately. I don't know how I slept because at the time there was so much on my mind. All I seemed to do in those days was worry. The problems stemmed from my recent leave. I had spent every day of the leave with Farida, either at her parents' house or at my mother's. One weekend the two of us had sneaked up to Genting. She took off her *tudung* and we slipped away, just the two of us. We checked into the hotel – we were Mr and Mrs Mahmud. In the morning and for the rest of the day we did all those romantic things we were supposed to do – we held hands, we snuggled up in the cold and we went for a boat ride on the lake. Then we slept together; but I just couldn't do anything. I had all sorts of excuses – 'We weren't married', 'I was scared' – you name it, I said it. She was very understanding; she kissed me so sweetly and said, "Don't worry." She's very fine like that. I was too embarrassed to say anything. She had some kind of inner strength that made it all okay, though I did catch her looking at me strangely now and again and then I returned to Sabah. I was so relieved to be back in Sabah, but the incident with Suriya was to haunt me for weeks.

Suriya didn't seem disturbed by our night together: she cooked, washed, cleaned and then disappeared on her Sunday off, as if nothing had happened. I wanted to talk to her, to explain to her and ask her not to say anything. And though I, too, carried on as if nothing had happened, I was afraid that she'd tell the workers, that they'd laugh and make fun of me. I watched her closely whenever I could but she didn't seem to have altered in her behaviour towards me and I was relieved: her hands still danced and her *baju* was just as tight as ever.

I was still afraid that she might say something, betray me and the thought of it, the anxiety, drove me out of the house that weekend. I ended up at the Club where I joined Jimmy and the rest of them. We hit the bars, each of us picked a girl – mine was called Esther – and headed off into the rooms at the back. I gave mine twenty ringgit and told her to keep her mouth shut. She counted the money carefully and stuffed it in her bra. I told myself that I was too worried to do anything more, too on edge. We returned to the Club and drank more until Chan kicked us out.

I drove home that night, drunk and bleary-eyed. I crawled out of the jeep and stumbled onto the verandah, where I collapsed in a heap as the drink, the anxiety and exhaustion finally overwhelmed me. Minutes later, I heard voices and two figures came towards me. I recognised Suriya. There was a young man with her who I'd never seen before. They half-lifted, half-dragged me to my bedroom where they undressed me first and then dropped me on the bed. It was a delicious feeling as these hands ran across my body undoing buttons, tugging at trousers and shorts. It was as if I was a child again and I distinctly remember that one pair was rougher than the other and that it was that pair that seemed to linger the most. I think I begged her not to say anything, but I don't really remember. After that I lost consciousness.

I saw the young man again in the morning. Suriya introduced him as her friend. He looked straight into my eyes and smiled as he was introduced and I remembered the hands from the night before. There was something very knowing about the way he looked at me and I turned away. I felt he recognised things in my eyes that I didn't want revealed. He was very dark and shorter than Suriya with a square-shaped head and a lean body – every muscle was clearly defined along his arms. He was in his early twenties and could have been an anatomical dummy for biology class. He wore a threadbare *sarung* and a white singlet that exposed the lines of his chest, his neckbones and his powerful arms. Even now, I can still remember tracing the line of his muscles along his arm.

Suriya smiled as she saw me looking at him. "Anton is to be my assistant," she said, knowing full well that I wouldn't disagree. And he smiled softly as I nodded, raising his eyes to meet mine. They were knowing and intense.

For the next few days I hardly left the estate. I would rise even earlier than normal and finish my rounds as soon as I could, returning home for lunch as well as for afternoon tea every day. Anton would serve me, laying the table and preparing my food. He'd kneel down to serve my tea, and I would look down his faded singlet, catching sight of his chest. Having served the tea he would pad around the house softly. I would pretend to be reading my newspaper but I couldn't help but watch him as he moved about me. He walked on the balls of his feet and like Suriya his hands always seemed to be dancing. I tried to concentrate on the newspaper or the radio but whenever he entered the room I watched him. It seemed as if he was a giant cat, a tiger and I his prey, because he seemed to stalk me, pacing around the rooms, his dark body sheathed in his tightly drawn *sarung*.

After the third week, I was beginning to lose sight of everything beyond the confines of the estate and calls from the neighbours went unanswered. I found every excuse possible to stay at the estate, missing all the functions at the Club. I spent all my time working on the accounts or checking the books; the books were open but to be honest, I didn't do a thing. Anton continued to prowl at night, slipping in and out of my bedroom as I undressed for bed – handing me clothes as I changed. One evening he placed his hand on my shoulder as he dusted off a piece of dirt and I nearly fainted. Every time I closed my eyes he'd be there. I knew that I shouldn't have allowed him into my bedroom but it just happened and because I wanted him there so much I was powerless to say otherwise. It was as if he was slowly slipping under my skin. A week later he entered the bathroom as I showered and stood there with a towel ready to dry me when I finished.

I tried slipping away from him but he was like glue; he stuck to me. He followed me from room to room, fetching water before I knew I was even thirsty, turning on the fan and adjusting the speed if I looked discomfited. I tried reading Farida's old letters over and over again, repeating her endearments like phrases from the Koran. I hoped they'd help, that they'd be some kind of talisman against the boy.

Each time he stepped close to me I would move away. And if he got too close I would try to look him directly in the face, catch his eye and then talk to him: man to man. I thought it would be better for me if I established a formal relationship between the two of us. Then at least there would be a barrier between us, something that would remind me at all times that he was a servant and a Filipino, and nothing more. In this way I'd prevent something happening, prevent the catastrophe that seemed to be about to take place.

I asked him about his home – he came from Zamboanga – and his family – there were fourteen of them. Initially he was shy but as we talked – he in his Filipino-accented Malay – he grew quite voluble. He sat cross-legged, on the floor beside my armchair, in his *sarung* and singlet. I offered him a beer but he, knowing his place, refused. I asked all the questions and as I asked, I tried to think of

Anton as a child of poverty and ignorance, something disembodied and separate from my life and not this feral presence that prowled through my house.

"My father," he said without emotion, "he sell me because I was big already. He tell me 'Anton, you are a man now – you must do what Mr Lim say'."

"But how old were you, Anton?"

"Eight years old, Tuan. In the Philippines, in my *kampung*, Tuan, eight is old. Only the rich people can let their children play."

"And what did you do for the *towkay*?"

"He like dogs. I look after his dogs, I clean them and feed them. He had seventeen dogs."

"What happened after that? Where did you work?"

"He sell me to agent who bring me to Sabah, to Sandakan. I clean shoes in the market and gut the fishes. But the man, he want more and he sell me.

"My new master, he let me work in the house. He was good to me, at first. But the work not nice ..." and he shook his head.

"What do you mean?" I asked him but he blushed and shook his head as if wanting to forget whatever it was that he had had to do in the past. And I, understanding the need for secret and silent places in the heart, the quiet recesses where the private horrors are hidden, bit my tongue – guilty for having probed so deeply into the young man's past.

"I'm sorry, Anton," I said after a long pause.

"Tuan is good to me. I work for Tuan. I want to become Muslim like Tuan and work for Tuan forever. I follow Tuan to KL." I was surprised by the passion in his voice, the words crackled with desperation and looking down at him, I saw that he was staring at me, imploring me. He bit his lower lip as he looked up. His excitement touched me and I smiled despite myself. I felt needed, realising in the brief exchange that the attraction was mutual. But that scared me and I was sharp with him.

"That's enough, Anton," I said abruptly, afraid of the emotion I saw on his face. "Thank you, Anton, that will be all for tonight." He bowed his head and left the room, deflated.

But I continued talking to him every other evening – it seemed to be the only way of having him in the house without me feeling threatened by his presence. I toyed with the idea of keeping him out, of asking him to leave and I did one night.

"Anton, please stay in your room this evening, I have work to do. I cannot be disturbed." I tried to do my work but I couldn't. I tried but all I could think of was Anton and his desperate longing. I fidgeted and paced about so impatiently that the next night I called him back. And, like a pet dog, he came willingly enough. Every night was the same thereafter with Anton sitting with me, often until well past midnight. Finally, alone in bed, I would force myself to think of Farida; I would try to remember her smile, the way she tucked her hair away before putting on her *tudung*, and the gentle refinement of her manners, drifting off to sleep as I repeated 'Farida, I love you' over and over again.

In retrospect, I don't know what came over me but because of Anton I forgot about the rest of the workers. They had noticed the preference I showed Anton: nothing is private on an estate. They treated him differently, laughing and teasing him. At the time I thought nothing of it. Then, one day nearly two months after his arrival, when I was on my rounds of inspection, I came across a scrawled line of graffiti – 'Tuan *sundal* Anton' ('Tuan is Anton's bitch'). I was so shocked by the words that I scrubbed them off myself, spitting on the chalk as I tried to erase the letters. But the word '*sundal*' remained, faint and readable despite my efforts.

That night, he must have sensed my uneasy mood because he was very quiet after dinner. He remained silent as I pretended to read the newspaper. However, he must have misinterpreted the signs; maybe he thought that my silence was an indication that I was willing and ready.

"Does Tuan want a massage?" he said, placing his hand on my thigh. His eyes burnt through me.

"No," I shouted, pushing his hand off me. "No, not at all and get out of here, you little *sundal*! Leave me alone – I have work to do," I added with less agitation though the strain must have showed through my voice. Embarrassed, he withdrew. He kept out of my way for the next week, observing a respectful distance. Suriya started serving my dinner and my coffee again.

It was about then that I got a call from my neighbour, Varna, inviting me to his Deepavali party. I loathed Varna but I knew I had to go, that I had to get away from the estate. Every one of the workers seemed to be sniggering at me and Anton's sulking presence permeated the whole house. He was like a wounded animal that howled into the night. No one else, however, could hear his cry of pain except me and I chose to ignore it.

I'd never liked Varna and he thought I was a prig. He had been poaching workers from me and stealing the barbed wire fencing that I had bought to keep out the elephants, so relations between the two of us were already strained. He was as black as the night and I trusted him as much as I would trust the jungle at night. Still, I went. Sometimes I'm a fool. His Deepavali party was famous for the amount of whisky he shipped in – mostly smuggled in from the Philippines – and San Miguel beer. It wasn't a wives' kind of party and everyone went in the expectation of the booze and the broads because for that one night, he had hired the Triple Eight Club – shipping the girls in wholesale, like the booze.

By now, I was already beginning to acquire a reputation as something of a fallen man. The other planters were happy to see that I'd started drinking and they were getting fonder of me. They'd pat me on the back and act conspiratorial – 'Try the broads at 707', 'There's hot stuff at the Razzle', 'Fertiliser's cheap at Man Hing's'. Of course Khalid Apong from Sabah Perkasa Bank became a little more distant and cold as he observed my steady decline.

The party wasn't too bad. Jimmy Gan was there, cradling one of his guns and everyone was in high spirits. It was good fun and I liked being friends with the rest of the planters: liked being liked by them.

It was a great feeling and I enjoyed it. I even played around with some of the girls, putting my hand up their skirts and all that. They all seemed to gravitate towards me – I was the youngest and it was fun having all these tiny Filipinas stroking my hair and nibbling my neck. One slipped her hand into my pants and started playing with me. But I was so drunk I hardly noticed.

Well, suddenly in the middle of all this, Varna stormed into the main room, dragging a naked Filipina. She wasn't that young, though her body was tiny. All I can remember now was that she had crow's-feet around her eyes, her breasts sagged and that her nipples were enormous for such a small woman. He dragged her in and threw her on the floor.

"What do you want for this used bit of '*pantat*'? She's hot," he said and we all laughed. We laughed noisily at first and then nervously because the woman started whimpering like that dog I caught Maria with. Pathetic sobs punctuated by jolting breath. Since I was the closest to her I could hear her asking for his forgiveness – "Please, sir?" – but Varna wasn't having any of it. He was in a foul mood and there was spittle flying from his mouth.

"Here, feel it, it's still warm and she'll do anything if you buy her. So what do I have? I bought her for a thousand ringgit. I'll sell her for less – her *pantat*'s too loose to pay any more for."

And then they all started bidding. Two, three hundred ringgit, then four, four-fifty and five. Jimmy Gan stopped at five: "I can get two Suluk virgins for that price." Even I chipped in as they hit six hundred. Meanwhile the girl was being passed around the guys who were fingering her like an animal – opening her mouth wide and examining her teeth, sticking their fingers up her and sniffing. Everybody seemed to find it funny and we all laughed though one or two of the guys, the ones who had married Filipinas themselves, kept to the back.

It was just then as the auction reached eight-fifty that she landed on my lap, naked and sweaty with fear. Her breasts brushed my face and her nipples were pushed against my mouth. All of a sudden, I was reminded of being in bed with Farida and Suriya. There was the same smell, the same soft, yielding flesh and my impotence, my visceral fear.

Her skin was clammy and hot. Shaken by the unpleasant memory, I pushed her away with a start, and she fell to the floor. As she fell, she grabbed my legs and screamed. I was trapped. Varna lunged forward and struck her across the face with the back of his hand. It was a loud crack of a slap that sent her head back against the chair leg. Then he kicked her in the kidneys.

"You ugly bitch. You are mine. I bought you fair and square. Don't think you can run off just like that with your Filipino boyfriend. I'm your master. I own you." And he slapped her again over the head. A wave of nausea washed over me – I was revolted by the scene being played out in front of me; by Varna and his Filipina. But it was more her, her touch against my body, her sweat and her fear. I felt as if she was trying to trap me and pin me down, like Farida and Suriya before her and all I could think of was how to escape. I hardly noticed Varna's tirade though I stood up and shouted at him. I think I said he was a bastard, but it was her that I was angry with, her – this limpet-like Filipina who was sucking the life from out of me, strangling me and holding me down.

Varna and the others ignored me. I tried to walk away but the girl wouldn't let go and Varna kept on hitting her across the face and swearing. There was spittle all over her hair, and blood.

"Let me go, you bitch!" and I, too, kicked at her, releasing my fear as I did. I pulled at her hair in desperation and a handful came free in my hand. I felt a searing pain in my leg. Looking down I saw that she had sunk her teeth into my shin. I reached down and with the full force of my right arm, I hit her square across the face. With that blow she was knocked halfway across the floor and I marched out of the room. I didn't return to the party but headed straight for my car and home. I never thought to ask what happened to the girl but she was never mentioned by the boys at the Club and anyhow a Filipina girl is easier to replace than a standpipe.

When I reached the house, I jumped out of the car and marched to the back of the house to Anton's quarters. I knew what I had to do; I had waited long enough, and stormed into his room. Without knocking, I pushed the door open. Anton was lying on his bed, reading a copy of *Variapop*. He must have heard me coming because he was smiling as I marched in.

"What is the matter, Tuan?" he asked. His eyes glowed with triumph. He laid there, his chest naked. Unmoving – taut and flexed. His body seemed all the more powerful and desirable: tightly wired and ready to uncoil at any moment. I looked away but turned back again. I couldn't look him in the face as I spoke; it was impossible. I knew what I wanted and I knew that he wanted me to take it. Still I couldn't do it and he, a servant at heart, knew only how to respond and not to initiate. "Nothing, nothing," I said and I walked out. All I could think of was the way his chest seemed to rise and fall as he breathed.

I slept alone that night. The next night, I went into town again, to the 707 and asked for the youngest girl they had. The mamasan said she was thirteen. Her name was Tita and she smiled like a child, cooing into my ear as she pulled the clothes from my body, folding everything up neatly as she went along. When I was naked I stripped her and let her play with me. I tried so hard to want her, I willed a response so fiercely that something did happen. Closing my eyes and lying back on my bed, I imagined the hands were not hers but Anton's. It was all Anton; his smell, his body and his cries. I dreamt so hard that even when she started moaning and pushed her tiny breasts into my face, the charade continued in my mind. But I had performed – I had passed the test I had set myself.

After washing I dashed off to the Club and stood everyone to drinks. I laughed with the boys and joked whilst Chan, the barman, looked at me strangely. I felt fully at ease among them for the first time, knowing then that I had solved for myself the only question that had separated me from all of them. I had no more questions now: I knew everything I needed to know.

I sang in the car on the way back to the house and laughed at my own foolishness. All it was, was the right woman: it was so simple, so clear. And I laughed again, amazed at the lightness in my head. I think I sang all the way back to the house, through the dark, oil palm-lined roads, like a madman. I had the answer, the solution to all my problems.

As soon as I arrived home, I called Suriya to the living room and told her to sack Anton. Puzzled by my sudden change of mind, she asked me if I was sure: *"Betul, Tuan?"* I repeated my instruction clearly and then walked into the bedroom. I had learnt something that had freed me from all my problems. I laughed again and took my shower, safe in the certainty that I knew, I knew. I, too, no longer had need for any more questions.

Neighbours

Datin Sarina prided herself on being well-informed. She was always the first to call her friends, sometimes even her enemies, with the latest bit of news. News, mind you, not gossip. There was a difference. The first was confirmed and therefore true whilst the second was unconfirmed and possibly untrue. Untrue at least until it was confirmed and to be quite honest it couldn't be confirmed unless it was repeated a few times.

She was also very proud of her ability to ferret out the truth, however unpleasant. Ignorance and stupidity were insults to Allah: the truth was always worth fighting for. For example, she had been the first to alert the world to Tengku Mizan's second wife, an achievement she regarded as equal to her husband's 'hole-in-one' the year before at the Golf Club. She had seen the girl, Aida, at Habib Jewels. The face was, of course, familiar to her: Sarina was an avid reader of *URTV* and *FAMILY* – she knew her artistes; her Wann's, her Ziela's and her Jee's. She'd sidled over to where the girl was sitting and watched her pick over the expensive trinkets, opening her ears wider as the girl lisped her husband's name.

When she saw the gold supplementary credit card she knew her research was done. She dashed home and called all the ladies in her circle. She spared none of the details, regaling them with the size of the diamond, "don't play the fool: two carat, you know?", her scent, "Giorgio *satu botol* – smelly!", the thickness of her make-up, "like elephant skin-*lah*" and the shortness of her skirt, "no shame can see her buttock!". Proud of her sleuthing abilities she relished her nickname, *Radio Sarina*.

Sarina was forty-five years old, romantic by disposition, shortish and a little too plump to be good-looking. As if to compensate for her stoutness, she liked to think she was voluptuous. She wore the loudest colours possible, shocking reds, turquoises and vermillions and tottered around on four-inch heels. She wore make-up at all times, serious jewellery for at least eight hours a day and exercised sparingly. Married to Dato' Mus, a civil servant ten years her senior, the couple had three children, all of whom were now studying abroad. Her husband's busy schedule and the children's absence had forced her to find other sources of entertainment, if only to stave off boredom.

Which was why it came as such a pleasant surprise when she heard that the house next door had finally found a new owner. It had been deserted for the past three years and she relished having neighbours once again – if only to have someone new to talk to and about. According to the estate agent the people were called the Kassims and they were from Penang.

Patient as always, she waited for the newcomers' arrival. And what a move. Lorry-loads of furniture and fittings arrived, followed by contractors and their workmen. The next few days were a riot of comings and goings as lorries, vans, cars and motorbikes unloaded all manner of people and goods. It was only when she was making an inventory of the furniture, totting it all up in her mind that she realised how much time she had spent looking at her neighbours. She was suddenly conscious of how wrapped up she had become in the Kassims.

It was all very well to be nosy about people like Tengku Mizan: they deserved all that was coming to them. Besides, everyone knew Mizan – his inability to keep his hands off big-breasted women was legendary. However, interest in the Kassims and people like that was a different matter; it was a bit embarrassing really. They were nobodies. It served no purpose – she couldn't talk about them to her friends. After a great deal of thought she decided that her interest in the Kassims had been a little extreme. However, it was educational – she had to learn about everybody. She shouldn't limit her interests.

Hastily then, she decided she should be a little more disciplined about these things. So she ignored the house next door, exercising a noble restraint when the servant girl came running to her one evening to tell her that the family had arrived to look at the house. Instead of rushing off to have a look at her new neighbours, she retired to her bedroom, drew the curtains and went to sleep. Self-control was very important in these matters.

She continued to treat the arrivals, then, as a temporary distraction, one that would be absorbed and made familiar in good time. This she considered was the correct way for a lady in her position to behave. Of course, the occupants of both houses soon made their own introductions. Her broken-tailed pariah cat Chomel impregnated one of her neighbour's silvery Persians very noisily late one night. And her own servant girl Amina, who was, it must be said, irrepressibly flirtatious, had done her utmost to get herself impregnated by the neighbour's surly chauffeur.

It was some time, however, before the heads of the respective households actually met. Sarina well understood the trials of house-moving and chose, she thought, once again with great restraint not to impose herself. One particularly hot afternoon she did, in breach of her own personal sanction, send cold drinks over to the house when she heard – through Amina – that the electricity had yet to be connected. Towards the end of the fourth week, and just after the *Isyak* prayers, Encik Kassim called at the gate, introduced himself and was invited in to have some coffee.

He was almost six feet tall. Somehow she had known he'd be tall. He was ramrod straight, smooth shaven, golf-tanned and smiling. Such a smile; she was quite disarmed. He couldn't have been more than thirty-five years old and was well-dressed – he was wearing a well-tailored pair of pants and a pink polo shirt that set off his healthy colour. Sarina felt a tremor of excitement as well as irritation with herself for not seeing him earlier: her new neighbour was so very good-looking. She was a little lost for words at first. But Kassim smiled again and, as if aware of his effect on her, made himself quite comfortable without troubling her. He was just so athletic, so attractive. She couldn't wait to tell her sisters: they'd die of jealousy.

Mus and Kassim soon dispensed with introductions and started talking about business. He said he was a lawyer and she was even more impressed. She slipped away into the kitchen as they started discussing market capitalisations, PE's, flotations and hot tips, subjects that always bored her. Once in the kitchen she prepared coffee for her husband and her new neighbour.

Arranging the coffee service on a silver tray, she marvelled at the splendour of this, her 'everyday' coffee service. She felt sure that the charming Encik Kassim would notice the fine quality of the porcelain. She could imagine the expression on his wife's face when he, as she felt sure he was bound to, described the thick gold inlay of the saucers and the delicate transparency of the cups. His wife would be jealous, envious and not a little flattered to be living next door to people of such distinction and quality. There were times when she felt that she was one of a dying breed: a Scarlett O'Hara in a land of pygmies.

Placing the tray down on the small side table between her husband and the visitor, she glanced at Encik Kassim, expecting him to exclaim aloud, 'Allah, what exquisite porcelain you have, Datin. Could it ... could it be Noritake?' But he didn't, at least not initially. She was unsure that the men noticed her departure. As it was, the two men had progressed from business to religion.

"... Datuk, these people they say that it's our duty to intervene and direct those who are transgressing the Koran. Well, I think that's wrong. Islam brings all men together under the guidance of Allah. We are beholden to Him to live as closely as we can within the dictates of the Koran. That doesn't mean that we should force the unwilling ... Oh, two sugars please, Datin, thank you very much. What nice coffee cups, Datin."

Sarina looked on admiringly as he drank his coffee; she was going to like this young man. He was so observant and such a gentleman. Didn't even slurp as he drank his coffee. Even Mus was beaming: Mus enjoyed a good theological debate and he was pleased to have a similarly inclined neighbour.

"Encik Kassim, you are so right. These preachers would have us living in the desert sands. The spirit of observance is of most importance, not mere outward display. There are many ways of serving Allah and it is important to allow each individual his right to chose his own way, and his own time within the dictates, as you say, of the Koran and the Hadiths."

She watched Encik Kassim closely. He had a handsome sculpted head, a large forehead – he was a lawyer, after all – and brown eyes. Oh, if only she was young again, she thought, only to be shocked by the impropriety of her thought. Kassim nodded politely as Mus made his points. Such nice manners. Observing him so closely, she felt sure she knew him or at least his family. It didn't seem possible that she didn't know him. He was obviously far too polished to be just anybody. She couldn't help liking the way he deferred to her husband and smiled so pleasantly – there just weren't enough nice young men around like this Encik Kassim. If he hadn't been married she would have rushed out and called all her unmarried nieces there and then.

"… it is not of interest to me that you or anyone else might drink alcohol, gamble or commit adultery. There is, of course, only one figure to whom we all owe obeisance and that is Allah. I might possess views about your behaviour which I could voice, were I inclined to do so, just as you would be free to reject whatever I have to say. Similarly I am free not to have to act according to your interpretations of the Koran and the Hadiths – because interpretations are all that they are, neither wrong nor right, merely differing views pertaining to the same subject …" Once Mus started it was often difficult to stop him.

"We are no longer living in small Bedouin communities in the desert. Neither are we personally equipped to act as judge against our fellow man. To be a judge of men's morals, personal or public, is something quite different."

"Datuk, I cannot agree with you more. It may be every Muslim's solemn duty to seek to attain the purest state before the Will of Allah. But that doesn't empower us to be moral arbiters and judges ourselves."

"I'll leave the highest state of grace to those who know better," Mus replied cheekily. He was enjoying the discussion. "I always say," he continued, "that Allah has endowed me with a brain that allows me the liberty of making my own decisions as to how I should lead my life. And I have chosen rightly or wrongly to seek the humblest place in heaven and no more. In short, Encik Kassim, I am an ordinary mortal using the blessings Allah has given me, to ask the questions that Allah must have expected us to raise.

"Come, come, don't let me bore you with my talk. Drink your coffee and I will show you the garden wall that I was telling you about earlier." And with a broad sweep of the hand, Mus drew the conversation away from religion to the commonplace.

Having been silent earlier, Sarina spoke up. She was very keen to meet Mrs Kassim now. If the husband was this good-looking and well-brought-up, the wife had to be exquisite.

"Encik Kassim, I do hope that your wife will do me the pleasure of calling on me when the family has settled in. Please don't be afraid to ask for any help. I understand how very tiring it is to be moving house."

"I will tell her," he replied warmly and then added, "actually my mother says she is related to you, Datin; her mother is Datin's mother's cousin."

Sarina couldn't contain her excitement.

"Oh, really, I should have known – you seemed so familiar. How interesting. Mus we're related! You must be Tok Su's *cucu* then? I remember now!" Mus smiled as well. She knew he was as pleased as her.

"I can assure you that my wife will call around as soon as she can. She would have come with me tonight, but her mother was not feeling well, so she had to go to Damansara Heights."

"Come, Encik Kassim, I'll walk you out. We can have a look at this troublesome wall." The two men stood up and walked out into the garden, where the shadows cast from the street lights drew patterns across the damp lawn. Sarina watched as the two figures, both so tall and poised, passed through the streaks of light, disappearing and reappearing. And as she watched them growing shadowy and dim in the dark she realised that from a distance it was hard to tell the difference between the two men. 'What a pleasant surprise,' she thought to herself as she cleared away the coffee things in preparation for bed. 'Such a nice young man, and a relative, too.'

The next morning, after her prayers, Sarina chose to watch the sunrise – a special luxury that she allowed herself now that her children had left home. As she sat, quiet and composed on the verandah outside her bedroom, she tried to think about the household. But try as she might she couldn't help but think of Encik Kassim. Visions of him flashed through her mind. And, if she was honest, it was because of Encik Kassim that she was now sitting on her verandah. Her verandah afforded her a view of her neighbour's master bedroom and whilst she tried to pretend to herself that she was enjoying the cool morning air, she couldn't banish entirely the real motive for her early morning vigil. Thoughts of the young man had swirled through her dreams all night long and as soon as it was possible she had arisen and taken her place on the balcony.

Just then, she noticed a light being turned on in the room opposite her verandah. The previous owners, a nice Chinese family called Teh, had known that anyone who had a mind to, could see into their main bedroom if the light was left on. As a consequence they had been scrupulous in their use of curtains when getting changed. Of course, the new occupants were not to know and Sarina, realising this, had waited patiently on the verandah. She knew that she ought not to sit on the verandah now, but the prospect of seeing Encik Kassim again enthralled her too much.

The first streaks of sunlight began to tell upon the lawn, airily slicing the dawn mists. Even without Encik Kassim, this was still her favourite time of day, and her reluctance to sit on the verandah drifted away much like the mists hanging over the garden. A delightful bluish tinge clung to the lawns now damp with the morning dew and swallows from the neighbouring trees swooped down to drink from the swimming pool. She had planted her garden with care, tending it lovingly over the years; the beds of heliconias had flourished and flowered, showering the garden with their crimson brilliance and dragon-like intensity. She never lost her wonder at their startling voluptuousness and the way they cascaded pod after pod. Alongside them she had planted pale silvery hibiscuses, ferns and more ferns. The garden was looking lovely and she let herself be lost in the play of colours and scents that surrounded her, forgetting for a moment her new neighbours.

Changing her mind once again she made a mental note not to glance over at the house opposite. She would enjoy the morning air and then return inside, deferring to the Kassims' modesty. She felt sure that *nice* Encik Kassim would understand. It was not uncommon for her to make such fine resolutions: not to talk about Raja Karina and not to spend too much of her husband's bonus. Inevitably, over tea at the Hilton or in her sister's house she would find the excitement of the occasion loosening her tongue and then, before she could stop herself, she had imparted to all assembled the truth about Raja Karina's little operation in Geneva or agreed to buy yet another set of diamonds.

Thus it was, that she pledged to herself not to look at the bedroom window of her neighbour's house whilst sitting directly opposite it. As was always the case with such situations Sarina felt defeated by surrounding circumstances. Here she was, trying not to be nosy, minding her own business as she enjoyed the early morning coolness, only to be thwarted by the Kassims next door, who insisted on leaving the lights on in their bedroom for all to see. She began to feel annoyed with the Kassims. After all, she thought, they must know that people could look in.

Maybe it was a deliberate act, some kind of deliberate oversight; maybe they were exhibitionists? Perhaps the young man wasn't as wholesome as he appeared? She laughed to herself: he was as wholesome as *ketupat*, just a million times better looking, that was all!

Maybe he was shameless? And she laughed again. Much relieved to discover that the fault, if indeed there was any, lay with her neighbours, she let her eyes settle on the room.

The room was entirely unadorned, spare and empty. There was a bed and a bedside table, no more. The wife, this Puan Kassim, was obviously not the sort of woman who cherished the small, poignant tokens of love – a family photo or bottle of scent. Having met Encik Kassim only the night before, she tried to create in her mind what she thought the wife would be like. Yes, she thought to herself, the wife must be exquisite but cold and hard.

Then, in the house opposite, the door opened from the bathroom and a woman entered the room. Her *sarung* was tied casually around her waist, her breasts exposed. Sarina was taken aback and with a jolt she turned her head away to face the garden, now mockingly enrobed in the gathering sunlight. Surprised by the sight, she determined to forget ever having seen it. She wanted to tear herself away from her vantage point, now shorn of the gentle, innocent pleasure it had once given her.

But she was unable to do so. Her curiosity had taken hold of her entirely and she felt impelled to look again: if Mrs Kassim was half-undressed, then maybe her husband would be too? Sarina was embarrassed by what she had seen, more angered by the invidious position that it had put her in. She wasn't a voyeur or a pervert. But look she did, and with a terrible avidity.

The woman was tall and slim with small breasts. Sarina felt a pang of jealousy at the woman's slimness – if only she had persevered with her diets. The woman had surprisingly powerful shoulders – shoulders that wouldn't have needed shoulder pads – and bedraggled hair that kept falling into her eyes though she tried to push it back. Because of the distance Sarina was unable to make out the woman's face clearly. But she thought her good-looking enough, with striking features and, like her husband, she was tall and erect – she had such bearing. There was a firmness and masculinity about her, emphasised in part by her lack of curves. She, this Mrs Kassim who wandered around her house bare-breasted, had no hips and thighs to speak of. The bearing of the woman, her pencil-slim shape and demeanour served to remind Sarina of the vast gap that separated the two of them. She was a woman of softer, older ways whilst Puan Kassim was stronger and more dynamic.

Mrs Kassim seemed unhappy. Her hands rifled through the bed clothes for some jewellery or underclothes. Sarina smiled to herself as she remembered similar fleeting encounters with Mus, and the men before Mus, meetings that had been snatched in between dances and dinners, baby-sitting and badminton. Those were in the days when sex had been something exciting for her and Mus. Now it was a chore as tiresome as dusting the furniture or washing the car, a chore that one underwent unwillingly with less frequency as the years progressed.

By now the light had reached its most perfect moment, lending a bronzed glow to all that it touched and she turned to her garden once again. The ranks of bougainvillea in her garden seemed to strain to receive the welcome warmth of the sun, so different from the harsher glare of midday. She had almost forgotten about Mrs Kassim as she watched, charmed and warmed by the steady illumination of her garden. Suddenly she felt the soft delicious cool of the breeze that curled its way through the suburbs, kissing her face as it passed by.

Mrs Kassim was sitting on the edge of her bed, applying cream between her legs. Sarina winced, both from the sight and from the memory of having had to do the same in the past. Then the woman started rubbing herself with greater rigour, arching her back and cupping her breasts with her free hand. Though Sarina had never herself masturbated, she knew that this was what Mrs Kassim was doing. She had been a little disturbed initially. She knew that she should have been shocked by what she saw but she wasn't and she carried on watching. She wanted to know as much as possible about this woman whose body shuddered with each stroke.

Just then another door opened and Encik Kassim came into the room. Sarina felt her own breathing quicken and she placed her hand on her chest, squeezing her own breast inadvertently. This was what she had been waiting for and she moaned silently. The wife did not notice him as she continued to stroke herself. Her strokes quickened and she shuddered violently. Encik Kassim walked around the bed until he was standing directly in front of her. Undoing his trousers he nursed his penis into her mouth. Sarina pressed her breast again and shivered.

She couldn't believe it! They were making love; this was far more than she had expected, though she couldn't say that she hadn't hoped for it. Even so she wasn't sure if she should be shocked or thrilled. Encik Kassim pulled off his trousers and underwear, throwing them across the room in his hurry. He leapt onto the bed and straddled it on all fours like a dog. She gasped and her hand dropped from her breast: what was he doing? He had a strong muscular back with just a hint of a paunch. His penis was monstrously enlarged.

The wife turned around and grabbed Encik Kassim firmly by the waist. Sarina could almost feel the bruises on his body. They were so violent and animal-like with one another! So, she thought, this was what it was like to make love passionately. She imagined herself for a moment in the place of Mrs Kassim, touching that young man and being touched by him. It was like one of those blue movies she had watched years before, only more real and more fervent. Her head was spinning with the possibilities.

Seductively and slowly the wife let her *sarung* fall to the floor. It slipped off her slim thighs and gathered in a pile at her ankles. Sarina swallowed hard; her mouth went dry. The woman's belly didn't taper off into a mound as her own did. The woman, or at least what she thought was a woman, had a penis of her own, a penis that was also erect. It was a *pondan*. She mouthed the word silently, a *pondan*.

'This can't be the wife!' she thought. 'No, surely not! How *could* he! He was so nice!' She didn't know what to think. He'd been such a polite and charming young man and a relative of her's as well – how could he do *this* … to her? It couldn't be! Her head spun painfully. She felt deflated and angry as if she had been let down. Encik Kassim had disappointed her, cheated her with his charming smile and his grey eyes.

The woman positioned herself behind Encik Kassim … her handsome Encik Kassim. Now she really was shocked, horrified in fact but still she watched, engrossed by the ugliness of it all. She was unable to pull herself away. But as she watched she became aware of the unnaturalness of what she was doing. Why was *she* watching? Why did she feel compelled to watch? Was there something wrong with her? Why couldn't she be like other people and mind her own affairs? Somehow she felt that it was her nosiness, her selfish persistence that had brought Encik Kassim to this.

Had she been more respectful of his privacy, none of this would have happened. She would have thought him charming and good-looking. Now he appalled her. It was all her fault, her responsibility. She had pushed him. Just as the thoughts rushed through her head the woman eased herself into him, shaking her head with pleasure.

She pulled herself out suddenly and slapped Encik Kassim hard across the buttocks as if he were a fat *kerbau* and sneered. And as she did, Sarina saw that he, *her* despicable Encik Kassim, moaned like a woman. He was no longer the man she had met the night before – sprawled across the bed like an animal, he seemed grotesquely subservient and feminine. The woman – she just couldn't call him a man, it was too monstrous – stood up. Encik Kassim moaned again and thrashed his buttocks in the air like a bitch on heat. Sarina wanted to retch. What was going on? She saw that the woman's features were hard and prominent like a man's. Did she have an Adam's apple? How had she missed it earlier? The woman turned the overhead light off.

With the light now off, Sarina realised that it would be possible for the couple to see her on the verandah. So, the blood draining from her face and terrified lest she be seen, she went back to her bedroom. It was a rare moment, a moment of shocking clarity. She could see herself as she was – the pretence and the falsity of how she lived her life had slipped away. Everything around her was sheared of its innocence. It was all a sham. She was a fat, overweight woman, neglected by her husband, whose emotional life was so thin and insubstantial that she could only find satisfaction in the private lives of others, a parasite who fed off the secret lives of others. She had nothing herself: she was nothing herself.

About the Author

Karim Raslan was born in Petaling Jaya, Selangor in 1963. Educated in both Malaysia and England, he is a graduate in English and Law from St Johns' College, Cambridge. Whilst at Cambridge, he edited the university's newspaper *Stoppress and Varsity* in the year it won *The Guardian/NUS Award for Best Student Newspaper*. Called to the Bar in Inner Temple, he spent some of his time in London writing leader editorials for *The Times* on north and southeast Asia.

He later returned to Kuala Lumpur where he practised in a large legal firm before leaving the profession to work on a novel which remains unfinished. After working for a few years as a freelance writer and editor for many newspapers, journals and magazines, including *The Business Times (Singapore)*, the *New Straits Times*, the *Far Eastern Economic Review*, *The Sun* and *Men's Review*, he returned to legal practice.

Heroes and Other Stories is his second book. His short stories have been published in *Skoob Pacifica Anthology Volume One: The Empire Strikes Back* and *Volume Two: The Pen is Mightier than the Sword*.

Also By Karim Raslan

Ceritalah: Malaysia in Transition
A riveting, intimate look at one of the world's
fastest-growing economic powerhouses
and its people.

"Elegant and educated." – V. S. Naipaul

"Work that breathes fire and ice over Malaysian
experiences." – *Business Times Malaysia*

"Essential reading." – *The Star*

The limousine-chauffeured *tai-tai* in Kuala Lumpur. The Penan hunter on the banks of the Baram river. The *pak haji* in Kota Bharu. Who is the real Malaysian of today? What are his hopes, his desires, his fears? Most of all, what does it mean to be Malaysian?

In *Ceritalah: Malaysia in Transition*, Cambridge-educated Karim Raslan probes and explores the psyche of a changing nation as it hurtles its way through both history and economics. Crisscrossing the country, he asks the vital questions that need to be asked and points to the many inconsistencies that still exist in present-day Malaysia. Always personal, always thoughtful, *Ceritalah* is a measured, insightful guide to an Asian dragon now redefining its role as the fulcrum of Asia.

Born in Malaysia, Karim Raslan has spent much of his life abroad. In between bouts of legal practice, he has written for numerous newspapers, magazines and journals, including *The Times* of London, *Business Times Singapore*, the *New Straits Times*, the *Far Eastern Economic Review*, *The Sun* and *Men's Review*.